Tl

D

By Hugh Morrison

MONTPELIER PUBLISHING

Published in Great Britain by Montpelier Publishing.
www.hughmorrisonbooks.com
ISBN: 9798536703380

The King
is
Dead

Chapter One

The little Fiat touring car bumped and slid its way along the appallingly maintained road that led through the far outskirts of Kecsprem, the capital of Fenekslavia. The night was bitterly cold, and the canvas roof of the car offered virtually no protection. The two men inside were bundled up in heavy overcoats, hats and scarves but both were shivering slightly, perhaps not only because of the cold.

The driver, a lean man of forty with a military bearing, a hawk-like face and a ruthless air, struggled to keep the car on the road while driving as fast as he could; silently he implored once more the protection of Saint Fenek, the country's patron.

The other occupant of the vehicle, perhaps ten or fifteen years the driver's senior, bore the unmistakable signs of someone used to good living; he wore an immaculately tailored overcoat, cut by Huntsman of Savile Row, and a homburg hat from Lock's; on his feet were shoes which might have appeared, to those unfamiliar with the craft of John Lobb of St James', to have been sculpted out of marble rather than leather. The desired effect was to appear as a perfect English gentleman; but of course, as anybody who has spent much time in England knows, absolute perfection in dress is the mark of the *parvenu* rather than the gentleman. This particular person was not fully aware of this distinction, as he was not English but Fenekslavian, although he had visited England often. He breathed on his gloved hands in attempt to warm them, and as he did so, he touched his jaw and lips awkwardly; he felt the unfamiliar sensation of clean-shaven skin where, only hours before, there had been a carefully cultivated and expertly dyed beard of the Van Dyke style.

The car passed the last of the long, low peasant houses, built of adobe and thatch, which lined the streets of the outer suburbs, and they were now in open country with no street lights to be seen. The driver took this opportunity to increase the speed of the car, which also increased its jostling and swaying.

'Curse this infernal jalopy, Zorard,' said the well-dressed man. 'It is giving me indigestion. Why could we not have taken the Rolls-Royce? Or the Bentley?'

The driver took his eyes off the road for an instant to flash a warning glance at his companion.

'I have told you, sir, please do not use my name until we are out of harm's way. And I have also told you that it is too risky to drive a large car – far too conspicuous.'

'Yes, yes, I suppose so,' said the well-dressed man. 'But since there are only about one hundred automobiles in the whole of Kecsprem, any car driving at speed at this time of night will be conspicuous. We should have taken the train.'

Istvan Zorard sighed and kept his eyes on the road. He glanced at the luminous hands of the small electric clock on the dashboard. They were in good time.

'We cannot cross the border either by car or train, sir. It is far too dangerous.'

'Then where on earth are we going?'

'I have arranged for us to travel by aeroplane.'

'By aeroplane? At night? But this is preposterous!'

'It will only be a short flight. An hour at most. I managed to find a pilot in the Air Force who is still loyal. He will fly us just over the border into Italy in one of the new German planes. It will cost dearly, but it will mean no border checks.'

'Well, well,' grumbled the man beside Zorard. He lifted an arm to adjust his hat lower over his eyes, and felt the enormous weight of his overcoat; a team of seamstresses had at short notice managed to sew a huge number of small gold bullion bars into the lining of his clothes, so that he was virtually armour plated. He glanced behind him to make sure the small holdall with its valuable contents was still there; it was.

'And you are sure my family is safe?'

'Yes sir. I have checked. Your son is well protected at the Prussian military academy, and your daughters are safe in Switzerland.'

'And my dear late wife is in the safest place of all, in the eternal embrace of the Mother of God. I am glad she did not live to see this.'

'Indeed, sir.'

'You have done well, Zo…I mean, my man. You did well also not to mention the aeroplane to me until now. I might have refused to accept such a plan. Well, it is too late now.'

'I am glad, sir,' said Zorard as he peered ahead through the windscreen at the winding road, lit only by the headlamps of the little car. 'Perhaps we ought to begin using the new name I devised for you.'

'A good idea,' said the man. 'Mr Basil George,' he announced carefully. 'Basil, because that is my Christian name, and George, because it is one of my middle names but also the name of the English patron saint. But is not George a Christian name, as with the English king?'

'I believe it can be both,' said Zorard. 'And I think it is safer than your original idea.'

'Ah yes, that was Mr Basil Piccadilly,' said the older man proudly. 'It has a good ring to it. Piccadilly is the name of the street in London on which the Ritz Hotel is located. I have stayed there several times as you know.'

'I do not think Your Maj… I mean, that you sir, should be named after a street,' said Zorard.

'You are right,' said 'Mr George'. 'Rather, it is the street that should be named after *me*.'

Zorard raised his eyebrows and shook his head slightly as he glanced over at Mr George, who had removed one of his gloves and was examining his fingernails.

Zorard looked back at the road and his eyes bulged; he shouted a Fenekslavian expletive and trod hard on the brake pedal. A light from a torch was being waved at them barely sixty feet ahead.

'What on earth now?' said Mr George, who had only just managed to avoid injury by grabbing hold of the dashboard with both hands.

Zorard peered into the gloom and felt for the pistol in his overcoat pocket. He saw two men in military uniform, both carrying rifles, standing by a little sentry box. A red and white striped wooden rail barred the road.

'Some sort of road block,' said Zorard. 'Curse it, I should have realised – the city limits checkpoint – it is usually not manned.'

'My God,' said Mr George. 'Turn this car around now, quickly.'

'It's too late sir,' said Zorard. 'To do so would attract

suspicion and we must not risk missing the aeroplane. They can't know who we are. Allow me only to speak, and do not use your pistol unless absolutely necessary, clear?'

'Very well,' said Mr George, who swallowed hard and pulled his hat a little further down over his eyes.

One of the soldiers walked up to the car while the other shone his torch through the windscreen, causing the occupants to blink and shield their eyes. Zorard turned to look at the man and recoiled as he smelt the man's breath, which reeked of the strong Fenekslavian spirit known as *poplinka.*

'Where the hell are you going so fast?' said the soldier, with slightly slurred speech. 'Didn't you see my torch?'

'An elderly relation in Premvec is at death's door, friend,' said Zorard. 'The priest telephoned and told us to hurry.'

The man swayed slightly and struggled to focus his eyes on Mr George, but finally he was able to get his words out.

'Priests…telephones…motor cars…swanning around like film stars…what sort of people are you?'

The other soldier, who seemed slightly less drunk, shone his torch further into the car.

'Papers, now,' said the second soldier.

Zorard handed over his identity papers and the soldier scrutinised them and handed them back. He then trained his torch on Mr George like a theatrical spotlight. Zorard felt beads of sweat start to appear under the band of his hat, and he swallowed hard.

'You as well, chum,' said the soldier to Mr George.

'How dare you!' spluttered Mr George. 'How dare you address me in the familiar! I am not your "chum"! This is disgraceful. That one is blotto and you are improperly dressed and unshaven. Do your collar up this instant.'

Zorard groaned inwardly. The soldier momentarily was lost for words, instinctively bracing up before the onslaught of someone used to being instantly obeyed, but then he caught himself.

'Who the hell do you think you are?' said the soldier. 'Capitalist swine. The days of you lot are over. Get out now.'

Zorard felt his hands twitching on the steering wheel; the drunken soldier crossed in front of the car to the passenger side and reached for the door. 'Yes, get out,' he slurred. 'Probably a Jew, by the looks of him. We'll show you who's in charge in this country now.'

Mr George's anger had melted away and he was cowering back in his seat. Before he had even a chance to implore Saint Fenek again, Zorard pressed down hard on the accelerator and the car sped forward, throwing the drunken soldier off balance. The flimsy barrier across the road shattered into matchwood as it was hit by the car's bumper.

'Halt!' shouted the other soldier, unslinging his rifle, and then his eyes widened in surprise as the car actually did halt. Zorard had stalled the engine.

'You're for it now!' shouted the drunken soldier as he picked himself up off the road.

'For God's sake drive man, drive!' screeched Mr George.

In that moment Zorard remembered to thank Saint Fenek that the car had an electric starter; there would have been no time to use a starting handle. He pressed it and the engine roared into life, and they were away.

The more sober soldier managed to fire one round, which pinged ineffectively off the car's back bumper; he then ran into the sentry box and rapidly wound the crank on the telephone. His drunken comrade-in-arms, shouting a string of curses at the disappearing car, managed only to jam the bolt on his poorly maintained rifle.

*

Two hours later, a group of men sat around a table in a room of the Royal Palace in Kecsprem, where the coat of arms of the sovereign had been hastily obscured by a red flag. The men, who had been summoned from the comfort of fire-sides and beds, were in various stages of undress, some with overcoats worn over their pyjamas.

'How was this allowed to happen?' said a man with a shock of grey hair angrily, banging his fist on the table. 'He must have been tipped off. There must be a counter-revolutionary amongst us.'

'Never mind how it happened,' said another man, who despite his unshaven face and unkempt uniform had the natural air of a leader. 'The important thing is that we find him, and in particular, what he has taken.'

'The capitalist swine,' said another man, who had not had to come in his night clothes as he had been found passed out in a tavern near the palace. 'We will tell the world that we will avenge. Nobody escapes the historical imperative of revolution.'

'That is exactly what we will *not* do, comrade,' said the unshaven man. 'Rather we will do the opposite; tell the world we no longer care. Good riddance to bad rubbish. Communism's new broom has swept Fenekslavia clean of kings and priests, and so on.'

'Preposterous!' said the grey-haired man. 'We must find him.'

'And find him we will,' said the unshaven man, 'but

the easiest prey is that which does not know it is being hunted.'

*

In an obscure back street in the Suffolk cathedral city of Midchester, Ana Walters began wiping down the café tables now that most of the lunchtime customers had left, and the slack period between now and tea-time had started. This was usually when she had a chance for a rest and to check on Sofia upstairs in the flat.

Her father-in-law and babysitter, Crispin Walters, although somewhat eccentric and luxuriantly bearded, did at least enjoy the company of his infant grand-daughter while he wrote his interminable tracts on vegetarianism, nudism, birth-control, pacifism, temperance, garden-suburbs and all sorts of other subjects. He had them privately published and placed for sale in the café, which annoyed Ana as she had to keep them clean. Nobody ever bought them, of course; the café catered for working men from the nearby riverside docks, who came in off the Thames barges which sailed up the Midwell, round the Channel coast from London. They came for the cheap filling food and that was all.

It was only thanks to her that there was even any decent food, thought Ana. Her father-in-law, a relic of the long-gone days of the Bloomsbury Set, liked to think he had the common touch and that he could influence the proletariat; but the proletariat were no more interested in Crispin's insipid vegetarian meals than they were in his pamphlets.

When it had opened in 1920 the novelty of a vegetarian restaurant in the provinces had attracted a few of Midchester's small circle of intellectuals at first; even the socialist poet Edward Carpenter had once visited while on a speaking tour, and his yellowing signed portrait still hung above the till where some less progressive businesses might have displayed a picture of the king.

Gradually, however, the intelligentsia had ceased to come as more and more rough working men had started to use the café, asking for sweet tea, bread and margarine or cabbage and potatoes, and 'none of that Indian muck'. That was what they called the rice and *dahl* that was Crispin's particular pride because it was said to be a favourite recipe of Mahatma Gandhi's.

'Thanks very much gerl,' said the last of the customers as he wiped his mouth with his hand, a rough looking working man, who nonetheless touched the peak of his cap and flicked a threepenny bit into the tips bowl on the counter.

'Thank you my friend,' said Ana with a smile, and closed the door behind him. She knew that part of the reason for the increased popularity of the café was not only the improved menu based on the blander varieties of Balkan peasant cuisine, but also the presence of an attractive young woman serving the food, instead of her father-in-law with his beard and green corduroy suit, who tried to engage the customers in conversation about his pet topics.

Only Ana and her husband Keir were now in the café. Keir sat as usual by the window, dressed in threadbare tweeds, smoking innumerable Woodbines and reading the *Daily Worker*. The title puzzled Ana, as since they had settled in England, Keir never seemed to actually do any work.

He was always going to see men about jobs, but nothing ever seemed to materialise. He had inherited most of the reforming zeal of his father, but with an edge of bitter realism forged in war and Soviet revolution (he had experienced neither, but had read extensively about them) and he considered his father a romantic Liberal.

Ana sighed and sat down opposite her husband. It was one of those murky English mid-winter days she had come to dislike intensely; days where it never really got light and the darkness set in around 3pm, so different from the clear, crisp winters of her native country. She caught sight of herself in the café window which had now become a mirror as the light faded in the street beyond.

At 25 she was by any standards beautiful, particularly by the standards of a down-at-heel English provincial town. Her slim figure had not been affected by the birth of Sofia, and the allowance from her father-in-law enabled her to have her raven hair cut and set regularly; she was even able to afford clothes from the cheaper outfitters in the city, whose wares would be beyond the dreams of the girls in the village where she grew up.

Keir, she thought, seemed not to have fared so well. The enthusiastic young English teacher with blond hair and piercing blue-grey eyes she had met two years ago had become jowly and unkempt, tarnished by the struggle to find work that he thought was fitting for him. The lines on his forehead and around his mouth had deepened as bitterness had set in; bitterness against every symbol of the British establishment from the King-Emperor George the Fifth down to the local postman when he failed to bring good news about a job application.

They had met in Fenekslavia when Ana had started taking English lessons. Her great dream had been to move to America, which her cousin in Baltimore told her was the land of opportunity; but for America, one needed to learn English. Lessons were expensive, however, so when she saw the advertisement for a native English speaking teacher who only charged 12 *lopeks* per hour, it seemed too good to be true.

She soon learned why it was so cheap; Keir had no qualifications and no great talent for teaching English; it was a way of making pocket money to finance his travels around Europe. His method, such as it was, consisted mainly of wandering around his room picking up objects and naming them in English, after which Ana had to repeat the word and write it in her notebook. During the lesson he would knock back large glasses of cheap red wine and then begin discoursing about his life in England, particularly his disillusionment over the failure of the General Strike to bring about a socialist revolution.

Ana struggled to understand at first, but, largely through her own efforts to study the language at home, she gradually started to appreciate what he was saying. She found it strange that he spoke so disparagingly of a country she had only heard good things of; but it seemed that rather than being the land of genteel lords and ladies from the story books, England was a country of decadent aristocrats, petty middle-class functionaries and bovine workers too stupid and lazy to rise up against their oppressors. But there was something about his foreign voice, the passion in it…were not the English supposed to be devoid of passion? She was soon to learn this was another misconception.

One afternoon, as the stifling heat of the Balkan summer threatened to overwhelm her with sleep, she interrupted Keir's monologue on something – coal miners, perhaps – by saying in faltering, but clear English:

'I love you. I don't…help it. I *love* you.'

Keir had looked at her dumbfounded and she thought he was angry that he had been stopped mid-flow, but instead he stood up so quickly that his chair fell over, and he embraced her. The result, she learned a few weeks later, was to be Sofia.

After some token resistance from Keir about marriage being an unnecessary bourgeois institution, they became man and wife in a brief ceremony in the town hall nearest Ana's home village. Then, to England and Midchester, where the industrious Ana started to revitalise her father-in-law's café with traditional meatless recipes from her home country which proved popular with the locals.

At first it was supposed be just a stepping stone on the way to America, but it seemed now that might never happen. America had become harder to get into, and it seemed Keir had something against that country as well as his own. Ana sighed and stood up. It was time to boil the urn for the afternoon tea customers.

'Blast them all,' said Keir, taking a Woodbine out of the packet and lighting it.

'What is the matter?' asked Ana.

'Public schools,' said Keir, squinting through the haze of blue smoke that poured upwards from the end of the cigarette in his mouth.

Ana remembered that Keir disapproved of public schools for some reason, though she could not remember what.

'There's a teaching job here,' said Keir, pointing to the newspaper. 'Would just suit me. English master. School certificate required. Three pounds a week.'

'That is a good salary,' said Ana. 'Why don't you try?'

Keir sighed. 'First of all, I don't work for a salary. I work for a wage. Working men work for a wage.'

'I will try to remember.'

'Good girl. And secondly, it's a blasted public school. In the *Daily Worker*! Alright it's probably very minor. Might even be one of those progressive ones. But still, I can't possibly work in a fee-paying school. Education is a right, not a privilege.'

'If we had three pounds every week,' said Ana, 'as well as money from your father for working in the café, we would soon have enough to get to America.'

'Hmm,' said Keir. 'Perhaps something will turn up tomorrow.'

'You say that every day,' said Ana.

Keir turned a page of the newspaper. 'Good God,' he said. 'Look who's crawled out from under his stone.'

He tapped a page of the newspaper which contained an article headed with a picture of a sleek, olive-skinned man in his fifties.

'Him!' spat Ana. 'Read it to me. I still find newspapers a bit difficult.'

Keir straightened the newspaper and began to read out the article. '"Liberation for the Feneks: King Basil II of Fenekslavia driven into exile following uprising of the workers." Well, we knew that was bound to happen eventually. You can't go on robbing a country blind like his lot were doing before the workers have had enough. It's the historical imperative.'

'The history what?' asked Ana.

'Never mind,' sighed Keir. 'Anyway, that's the good news. Here's the bad news. Old Basil's coming to England.'

'He should have been killed in a cellar like the Czar,' said Ana, bitterly. 'He was the one that refused to, how you say, forgive my father.'

'Pardon him, you mean,' said Keir. He remembered that Ana's father had been court-martialled in the war for refusing to lead his men to certain death against the enemy's guns, and a specific plea by the court to King Basil for clemency by Ana's mother had been personally turned down.

He read on. '"The exiled king, who narrowly escaped trial by a citizens' tribunal by fleeing the country by air last week, is thought to have settled in the east of England near the village of Lower Addenham, posing as a bourgeois country gentleman. It is not known if he intends to remain in this country, as there have been moves by reactionary forces to form a counter-revolution. Those wishing to financially assist the Fenekslavian Workers' Soviet should send a cheque or postal order care of, " etcetera etcetera etcetera.'

He put the paper down and stubbed out his cigarette in the tin ashtray next to him. 'Well Ana, it looks like a little piece of our dear Fenekslavia has arrived in reactionary old England, and somewhere near here, too, though God knows why.'

Ana's eyes flashed an ancient Slavic fury which even her husband, used to her moods, found unsettling.

'He robbed and cheated our people for years,' she said, 'and did not show mercy for my father. And now he thinks he can just run away? If I see that man I will kill him.'

*

A few miles away in the little village of Lower Addenham, Christmas suddenly appeared much closer. A light snowfall began to dust the half-timbered houses; the fairy lights in the George public house cast their tiny beams on the village green, which slowly became white.

A tall, slim man in fit middle age, with a fine head of iron-grey hair, watched from the window of the little Georgian vicarage opposite. He resembled, and in fact, had even once been mistaken for, William Inge, the 'Gloomy Dean' of St Paul's Cathedral in London; but he held no such high office, and was merely an ordinary country parson.

The scene began to resemble something from a Christmas card or the lid of a box of chocolates, thought the man, whose name was Reverend Lucian Shaw, vicar of All Saints' church. The only thing spoiling the romantic vision was the row of motor cars parked outside the George, which added a jarring modern note to a scene which otherwise might have taken place four centuries earlier.

Shaw drew the curtains as the light outside sank to a gloomy dark blue, as if the windows had been coated in Stephen's Ink. He had just finished his sermon for the following Sunday and wondered whether there was time for a pipe before Hettie served tea at five. He decided against it; a rushed pipe was pointless; one might as well take up the cigarette habit if one desired instant gratification.

Just then he heard the front door open and a woman's voice thanking Hettie. It was his wife, Marion.

Mrs Shaw bustled into the room. Though not what one might call beautiful, she was of the type sometimes referred to as a 'handsome', with a well-preserved figure and carefully coiffured dark hair that belied her age.

Beyond her in the little hallway he could see Hettie hanging up her mistress' large fur coat and cloche hat, and trying not to trip over various large boxes and parcels that had been left on the floor.

'Thank goodness I caught that train,' said Mrs Shaw,

kissing her husband on the cheek. 'Otherwise I would have had to wait another half an hour in the beastly cold, and they never light the fire in that waiting room at Midchester. I say, it's lovely and warm in here though.'

She warmed her hands at the little coal fire in the corner of Shaw's study. 'I thought you'd have a jolly blaze going in here. It seems such a waste to light one in the drawing room when you're never in there.'

Shaw smiled and stopped himself from correcting his wife about the use of the term 'drawing room', which he considered far too grand for a house of this size.

'Were the shops busy?' he enquired.

'Absolutely teeming,' said Mrs Shaw, slumping down into an armchair by the fire. 'I feel quite worn out, though I did manage to get most of the things on the list. Do you know, Christmas seems to get earlier every year.'

'Technically it is still Advent, but yes, it does seem so,' said Shaw. 'The shops also seem to say every year that this will be their greatest Christmas ever.'

'I rather thought that was the first one,' said Mrs Shaw, laughing. 'Oh sorry,' she said. 'I know you don't like religious jokes.'

'Only because most are of poor quality. That was quite a good one,' said Shaw. He looked at the clock in the corner. 'It's nearly five. Shall we ring for tea?'

'Oh do please Lucian,' said Mrs Shaw. 'I'm quite parched. That little place at Midchester station had run out of hot water – can you believe it – and had nothing to keep the wolf from the door except a few stale Banburys on the counter.'

Shaw rang the little bell on the chimney-piece.

'Ah, Hettie, you read my mind,' said Shaw as the maid entered with the tea things. 'Prompt as usual.'

'Very good sir,' said Hettie, placing the tray on the

small table by the fireside and laying out the cups. 'Shall I pour sir?'

'No that's quite alright, we'll manage,' said Shaw. 'Have a rest before dinner. I see you've been hard at work putting up the Christmas decorations.'

'Thank you sir, it seems to get earlier every year, doesn't it?'

'Indeed it does.'

Hettie bobbed and left the room. 'Oh, you do spoil her Lucian,' said Mrs Shaw. 'What's the point of having servants if one pours one's own tea?'

'In order that one might retain them, if nothing else,' replied Shaw. 'Hettie works hard and servants are extremely hard to come by these days. Good ones, anyway.'

'Of course you're right Lucian. I dread to think what things would have been like if that ghastly Mrs Talmadge had still been here. Shall I be mother?'

She raised the teapot over her husband's cup. He nodded his assent.

After both their cups had been filled and they were relaxing by the fire, Mrs Shaw, who had lapsed into drowsy silence, suddenly spoke up.

'I heard the most extraordinary thing on the train today,' she said.

'Oh yes?' asked Shaw cautiously with a raised eyebrow, wondering what minor parish scandal he was about to be made party to.

'It all came from Mrs Chadwick.'

'Who?'

'You know. Ronnie Chadwick's wife, they live at Well Cottage along the lane. That dreadfully High Church woman who's constantly crossing herself during Matins.'

'Ah yes,' said Shaw. 'She once asked me whether I

had ever thought of trying a *biretta*. I said I was not well acquainted with shotguns but had heard that Beretta was a reliable make. It turned out she was referring to the hats worn by our Roman Catholic counterparts.'

'Oh dear,' said Mrs Shaw. 'I do wonder why people like that don't just go the whole hog and actually go over to the Roman Catholics.'

'We are a broad church here,' said Shaw, 'and ought to accept minor differences in ritual. After all, these things are only outward and visible signs.'

'Yes I suppose so,' said Mrs Shaw. 'Anyway, before we go off on a religious tangent, I was going to tell you what she – Mrs Chadwick – said to me. You know that place called The Larches?'

'Is that the house where Major Chilcot lived?'

'That's it,' said Mrs Shaw. 'A sort of imitation Tudor manor that looks like one of those public houses one sees on the Great North Road. Awfully grand and not a larch in sight.'

'Yes, I remember it,' said Shaw. 'I took Chilcot's funeral last year. I don't recall him ever darkening the doors of the church but he left us a sizeable amount in his will.'

Mrs Shaw raised an eyebrow. 'I dare say he wasn't short of money,' she said. 'I can't imagine anyone poor living in a house like that. Anyway, you'll never guess who's moved in there now.'

'Indulge me.'

'Well, Mrs Chadwick's daily has a sister who is, or rather used to be, cook-general for Major Chilcot. His will apparently stipulated that she was to be kept on, on half pay, until the house was sold, and then she was to be employed by the new owners. All rather feudal, don't you think?'

'Quite,' said Shaw, trying to suppress a yawn. He could never really understand the female fascination for the minutiae of human relationships at all levels of society.

'I can see I'm boring you Lucian, so I shall get to the point,' said Mrs Shaw briskly. 'The house has been sold and you'll never guess to whom.'

'Please let it be a wealthy cinematograph actor who wishes to endow the church and open the fête every year,' said Shaw, looking upwards as he clasped his hands together in mock prayer.

'Even better,' said Mrs Shaw. 'It's a *king*.'

Shaw leaned forward in his seat and placed his tea cup and saucer on the little table.

'You mean some sort of industrialist? A scrap-metal king, or the like?'

'No, I mean an actual king. Well, an exiled one anyway. From somewhere in the Balkans I think. Or one of those places in the near east where they're always having uprisings. An Ottoman, or something like that. Or is an Ottoman a type of chair? I'm never quite sure.'

Shaw thought for a moment and then vaguely recalled a small item in the newspaper a few days previously. 'You mean King…Basil, of, er, Fenekslavia? Surely not.'

'If that's the fellow who was in the *Times* the other day then yes, it sounds like it must be him. But he doesn't call himself a king, according to Mrs, thing, the cook.'

'Yes, I recall now something about him renouncing his title. I think the Bolsheviks got rid of him. An all too common tale in recent years, alas.'

'But just think of it, Lucian. A king, in our little parish. What fun!'

'"The King is but a man as I am, the violet smells to him as it doth to me,"' quoted Shaw.

'Psalms?' queried his wife. 'No, it doesn't sound like

that. Something from the Apocrypha?'

'Shakespeare I think,' said Shaw. 'Or possibly Browning. No matter; my point is I wouldn't be too much in awe of kings and princes. I once shared a set with a Maharajah when I was up at Cambridge. His sole topic of conversation was his stamp collection.'

'Oh well,' said Mrs Shaw, swallowing the last of her tea. 'I think it's rather exciting.'

'Stamp collecting?'

'No, silly. I mean having a king in our midst. And don't start saying we have a heavenly king in our midst at all times or something. I know what you're like.'

'Forgive me my dear, but religious metaphor is rather my stock-in-trade. What I mean is, I fear this parish has had enough excitement for some time.'

'That awful business with the Cokeleys* you mean? Yes I suppose so, but this is a *nice* sort of excitement.'

'From what I recall of the newspaper article,' said Shaw, ' this man wishes to remain incognito. We ought to respect that. I expect he will remain hidden from view behind the half-timbered walls of The Larches.'

'I do wonder why he chose our little corner of Suffolk though,' mused Mrs Shaw. 'I rather thought these characters lived in mansions flats in Belgravia, playing bridge all day.'

'Probably because,' said Shaw, 'they are unable to leave the house without photographers from the society publications hounding them.'

'It reminds me of that king,' said Mrs Shaw. 'You know the one from Hungary, or was it Poland, that was exiled after the war. Didn't he end up on Madeira?'

'You mean he turned to drink?'

**See* A Third Class Murder

'Honestly Lucian, I can never tell if you are being serious or not. I mean he was exiled to the island of Madeira, not that he drowned his sorrows in wine. Although perhaps he did that as well.'

'I expect these exiled kings just want privacy, not a constant reminder of their lost status,' said Shaw.

'I suppose you're right, Lucian,' said Mrs Shaw with a sigh. 'It would be rather nice to find out a bit more about him though. And as vicar of the parish you're one of the few people who can just turn up and introduce yourself.

'Or so I should think. I say, do you know I've no idea what the form is with people like that? Do we leave cards with him or wait for him to summon us, or what?'

'Shall I check in *Debrett*?' asked Shaw with a smile. He knew his wife was a devotee of that manual of social correctness.

'Now you're teasing me,' said Mrs Shaw.

'Just a little, dear. However, it is not inconceivable that I shall be passing by The Larches at some point, and if I do I may just happen to make his acquaintance.'

Chapter Two

The stage manager stuck his head around the door of the dressing room, deep in the bowels of the Gaiety Theatre, Midchester.

'Half an hour please ladies,' he said, covering his eyes with his outstretched hand in a pretence of shielding his gaze from the sight of so many semi-clad women.

He withdrew quickly with a yell as a high-heeled shoe landed on his forehead.

'Oh do get out Len, we know what the time is, you just want a good look,' one of the chorus girls shouted as she slammed the door shut and picked up her shoe.

'Good shot Deirdre,' shouted another of the actresses as she snapped her suspender belt into place. This was followed by raucous laughter and then the room lapsed back into the nervous busyness and double-checking that takes place backstage in any theatre shortly before a performance.

One of the performers, Elsie Garnham, sat in a corner of the room away from the bustle of the other girls. She carefully checked her make-up in the cracked communal mirror surrounded by gaudy light-bulbs, some of them broken. 'Sure Shot Sue, England's Annie Oakley' she was billed as, a cut above the chorus girls but not quite top billing, so she did not warrant her own dressing room.

Her act consisted of taking pot shots at various moving targets on stage with a .22 rifle and pistol, using unusual positions calculated to show off her legs to their best advantage. This culminated in her pretending to accidentally shoot herself with a pistol and then miraculously coming 'back from the dead' at the end.

It had worked well for a while; she'd grown up with guns on her father's farm and then after a brief period in the circus had set out on her own. She wasn't stupid however, and both she and her agent knew the main attraction of her act was her looks rather than her firearms skill.

Pressing her lips together, she frowned and then made a final adjustment with her lipstick. She reached for her make-up case next to her, but found it missing. She turned to face the other girls and exclaimed angrily.

'Here, which one of you's pinched my make-up box?'

There were general mutterings of 'don't knows' and 'not me dears' from the other girls, which failed to placate Elsie.

'That case has all my theatrical make-up in it and I need that blood capsule for my death scene. Come on, who's got it? I've had that box ever since I started on the stage.'

'Must be a priceless antique by now then, dear,' said an unidentified voice from behind a clothing rail. Elsie pretended to ignore it.

'Is this it, Elsie?' said a young woman next to her. She revealed a small wooden case on the chair next to Elsie, which was hidden under a frilly dress. 'I'm ever so sorry, I put my frock over it by mistake. Here it is.'

Elsie eyed the young woman suspiciously.

'Thanks Violet,' she said, without much warmth. 'See that it doesn't go missing again.'

'Well...,' said Violet, 'I don't suppose it's likely to now, is it?'

'And what's that supposed to mean?'

'I mean to say...word's got around, like.'

'Word's got around about what?' asked Elsie, though she was pretty sure she knew what the answer would be. She looked at herself in the mirror; still attractive at 32, with a face and figure that, with the right clothes and careful make-up might still turn heads for another five years or so, but she couldn't count on it for a living.

She'd had offers of marriage before of course, but nobody had quite made the grade, until now. No, she thought, it was about time she packed all this in so she might as well come clean. She thought she might keep Violet in suspense a bit longer, though.

'Come on, what have they been saying about me?' asked Elsie, conscious that many of the younger girls on the chorus line would be keen to see her go. Well, she thought, they'll see me go all right, but it'll be a step up from a glorified provincial music hall like the *Gaiety*. She noticed the room had suddenly gone quiet.

'I've heard that...that you're leaving us,' said Violet. 'That you've got a chap.'

''Course she's got a chap, pretty young thing like her!' said a buxom blonde woman of about 19 whose name was Elspeth.

Elsie glared at her. 'Yes, I've got a chap and yes I'm leaving, if you must know. And don't sound too disappointed as you'll start me off crying and I don't have time to do my eyes again.'

'Is it...him?' asked Violet. 'The gent that took you out for supper every night when we was on the continent?'

It was impossible for gossip not to spread in a small variety troupe, stuck together in digs on a recent tour of little European countries whose theatres could not afford French dancing girls or American variety acts, and who had to make do with cheaper English ones instead.

'Some foreign fancy-man chasing you all the way to England?' asked Elspeth. 'Crikey, you must have handled more than a pop-gun to make him want to keep you.'

Elsie's kohl-rimmed eyes flashed fire at Elspeth and she felt her long fingernails digging into her palms as they formed fists. You'd better not slap her, she said to herself. Remember the last time? That girl's nose broken and you only getting away it by being nice to the producer. You can't afford any bad publicity now and besides, the producer this time's 'one of them' and you won't get far being nice *there*. It would be act one beginners soon anyway. She smiled sweetly at Elspeth.

'Actually dear, he's not keeping me anywhere. Matter of fact, he's asked me to marry him and I said yes.'

She reached into her handbag and slipped something on to her finger, then extended her arm dramatically so that her hand could catch the light. The women in the changing room gasped at sight of a ring topped with an enormous diamond.

'Oh Elsie, it's beautiful,' whispered Violet, looking at the ring as if it were a religious relic. Elsie quickly tucked the ring away into her corset.

'Well I never,' said Elspeth, who sounded grudgingly impressed. 'Suppose you must think you're the Queen of Sheba now.'

'No dear,' said Miss Garnham. She breathed deeply. Now to deliver the killer blow to that silly little bitch, she thought. 'Good guess though. Matter of fact, I'm going to be the Queen of Fenekslavia.'

*

The following morning in All Saints' church, Shaw concluded the daily office of Morning Prayer, as always, with the prayer of St Chrysostom:

'Almighty God, who hast given us grace at this time with one accord to make our common supplications unto thee; and dost promise, that when two or three are gathered together in thy name thou wilt grant their requests; fulfil now, O Lord, the desires and petitions of thy servants, as may be most expedient for them; granting us in this world knowledge of thy truth, and in the world to come life everlasting. Amen.'

He then pronounced the Grace more quickly than usual, given that it was bitterly cold and there was nobody in the church except for Simpkins, the warden, and a man sitting at the back behind a pillar, whom he could not identify. Normally at least one or two regulars turned up for the early morning daily service, but today there were none; the low temperature and the thin sheen of frozen snow on the paths had probably put off the handful of elderly men and ladies who had the time and inclination to attend church on a weekday morning.

'Thank you Mr Simpkins,' said Shaw, as he emerged from the vestry, putting on his overcoat for the short walk back to the vicarage. 'The mornings seem to be getting colder every day.'

'That they do, vicar,' said the warden. 'But there's no point getting the verger to start the furnace just for the daily office. Place will be only just getting warm by the time you've finished.'

'Yes, quite,' said Shaw, who was aware of the cost of coal required for the leaky church heating system, fifty years out of date. 'Still, put on the armour of light, and all that.'

'That and a good pair of woollen combinations under it,' said Simpkins with a chuckle as he walked home across the churchyard.

There was a chill wind in the air and the low, lead-grey sky held the promise of future snow. Shaw, alone in the churchyard, breathed in deeply and enjoyed the smell of the English countryside in winter; the crisp aroma of chilled earth with a hint of coal smoke drifting over from the village. He looked forward to a walk in the woods after breakfast with Fraser, his little West Highland terrier.

Then Shaw realised he was not alone. A man emerged from inside the church.

'Very nice service vicar, and a nice warm church too,' he said. 'Well, warmer than out here, anyway.'

Shaw looked at the man and his heart sank slightly. The scruffy looking, unshaven individual was twisting his cloth cap in his hands. Shaw realised it was Griggs, an itinerant worker, a tramp really, who usually spent the winter months in workhouses or prisons, occasionally turning up to cadge small amounts of money.

'Ah, good morning, Mr Griggs,' said Shaw. 'No winter quarters for you the moment?'

'Yes vicar,' said Griggs. 'I got digs with a farmer here. He's waiting for a lorry supposed to be taking firewood to Ipswich. Been promised a job on it.'

Griggs always seemed to be waiting for a man, a lorry, or a place to live. Shaw guessed what was coming next, so he pre-empted it.

'If you are in need of work, the snow ought to be

cleared from the church path. Shall we say a shilling a day until your next job begins?'

'Ah, well now vicar,' said Griggs, with an uncomfortable look on his face, 'I can't risk starting a job as I can't finish, in case this lorry comes along. I was wondering if…'

'Unfortunately Mr Griggs the church is unable to give out money, as you know. The Outdoor Relief office in Midchester may be able to assist you. A bus leaves from here shortly.'

'Ain't got the fare though, have I vicar?' said Griggs, with a knowing smile.

Shaw sighed and took sixpence from his pocket. 'Here you are. Pay me back once you get your job.'

'Right you are vicar, God bless you.' Griggs touched his forehead and loped off in the opposite direction to the bus stop, towards the village stores where Shaw reflected wryly that rough cider was available at sixpence a jar.

Shaw heard the rumble of an engine and looked up the road to see than an expensive looking car – a Rolls-Royce, as far as he could tell – had pulled into the little gravelled carriage turn of the vicarage.

Shaw walked to the front door of his house and admired the vehicle. A little grand for Suffolk, he thought. He opened the door and stepped into the little hallway. Hettie was already there, looking flustered.

'Oh sir, I'm glad you're back,' said the servant. 'There's someone to see you. I told him you were at church but he insisted on waiting to see you so I showed him into the drawing room, I hope that's all right.'

'Yes, quite all right, thank you Hettie,' said Shaw, as the servant helped him off with his overcoat and hung it on a peg. He noticed an expensive looking fur-collared overcoat and a black trilby hat hanging there.

'He left this,' said Hettie, handing Shaw a visiting card. 'I've no idea what it says sir, it doesn't seem to be written in English.'

Shaw took the card. Marion, he thought, had claimed to have taught Hettie the protocol of presenting a calling card on a silver tray, but he declined to mention the lack of this as he could see the girl was nervous.

He looked at the card; there was some writing on it which looked as if it were Czech, or perhaps Hungarian. He saw what must be the name in the centre of the card:

Vecšmetzemév
ZORARD
Istvan Stéfan Ivěnof

'Thank you Hettie, that will be all,' said Shaw. 'Would you tell Mrs Shaw that I shall be late for breakfast?'

'Very good sir,' said Hettie with a bob, and then disappeared upstairs to warn Mrs Shaw that her husband was occupied with a visitor.

Shaw stepped into the drawing room. He saw a tall, athletic looking man with dark, swept back hair and a small moustache. He was dressed in a well-cut double breasted suit, and stood by the window looking out into the garden. The man turned as he heard Shaw come in.

'Ah, Father Shaw, I assume?' Shaw took the hand proffered to him.

'*Mr* Shaw, actually.'

'Ah of course, my mistake,' said the man. 'It is the Catholics who are addressed as Father. I should have remembered.'

Shaw wondered whether to point out that some of his Anglican colleagues preferred the Roman Catholic title also, but decided it might complicate matters. The man seemed fluent in English, but spoke with a noticeable foreign accent.

'And you are...forgive me...' Shaw looked at the card and struggled to pronounce what was written on it. 'Mr Vecsmet...zev?'

The man laughed. 'Now we have both made a mistake,' he said. 'I have not yet had time to have cards printed in English. My name is Zorard, Istvan Zorard. *Vecšmetzemév* is my military rank. I believe it is equivalent to lieutenant-colonel in your country. But 'mister' is suitable also.'

'Very well, Mr Zorard,' said Shaw. 'Won't you sit down?' He gestured to the chintz-covered sofa by the window.

'Thank you Mr Shaw,' said Zorard. 'A beautiful room,' he said, looking around. 'Small, but elegant.'

'Indeed,' said Shaw. 'May I ask to what do I owe the pleasure of this visit?' He had an inkling of what it might be, and was, he realised, rather eager to find out if he was correct.

'I represent my...employer,' said Zorard, 'who has recently moved into the area, temporarily. His name is Mr Basil George, of The Larches house. You know of it?'

'The Larches? Yes, it is on the edge of the parish. I was acquainted with the former owner, Major Chilcot.'

'Quite so, quite so,' said Zorard. He took out a silver cigarette case. 'May I?'

'Of course,' said Shaw, declining the offered open case with a wave of his hand. Zorard lit a fat, round cigarette and the room was soon filled with the strange, incense-like scent of Balkan tobacco.

'I can see you are in suspense,' said Zorard with a smile. 'You may know my employer better by his proper title: His Majesty King Basil the Second of Fenekslavia,

Regent of the Holy Crown of Saint Fenek, Protector of the Slavic Cross, Duke of Transpredestia, etcetera, etcetera.'

'I see,' said Shaw. 'There were rumours that His Majesty had moved into the area.'

'Please,' said Zorard, 'my employer has asked that, while he is in this country, he will be known by a simple English name, that of Mr Basil George. And I am to be known as his private secretary, although in our homeland my title is much longer and difficult to pronounce.'

'Very well,' said Shaw. 'And how may I be of assistance to Mr George?'

'You may be aware, Mr Shaw, that it was necessary for Mr George to leave Fenekslavia in unfortunate circumstances. The Bolshevik menace has consumed our little country.'

'I read as much in the newspapers,' said Shaw. 'I imagine things are rather difficult for you all at the moment.'

'I am a military man, Mr Shaw, as was Mr George, we are not unacquainted with personal inconvenience; what is hard to bear is the desecration of the throne; to have to leave our homeland like thieves in the night, and live as ordinary men, scraping for money and having to live in a middle-class house, with barely any servants, not even a driver.'

Shaw was beginning to wonder if this was some sort of hard-luck story and he was being tapped for money just as he had been by Griggs a few moments earlier.

'Is there no support for you here?' he asked. 'Our own king, perhaps…?'

'I fear not Mr Shaw. My country had the misfortune to side with the Germans during the Great War. There is neither great interest in, nor affection for, my people here, even those of royal blood.'

'I am sorry,' said Shaw. 'The consequences of that war have reached further than most of us realise.'

'No matter,' said Zorard, stubbing out his cigarettes on the little Benares brass ashtray by the sofa. 'So then, to business.'

*

The little Morris Commercial van made its way slowly along the winding road between Midchester and Great Netley. It was cold in the unheated cab, and Ana drew a musty-smelling blanket tighter over her and baby Sofia. Keir, his neck swathed in a huge hand knitted scarf and with his cap pulled low over his eyes, lit a cigarette, steering the van with his knees as he fumbled with his matchbox.

'Blast this van,' he said. 'It's like Greenland in here.'

'We are lucky your father has this for the café supplies,' said Ana. 'At home nobody with a café like ours could dream of owning a van like this. He has to carry the bags of flour and such on a mule, or just a cart he pushes himself.'

'I suppose you're right,' said Keir, crunching the gears as he struggled to double-declutch on a tight bend. 'Only if father must send us out on these supply runs he might give us something a bit easier to drive. When I was a volunteer driver in the General Strike we had a Ford van. That was a joy to drive. It had a heated cab and…'

'Stop!' shouted Ana.

'What the…?' Keir stopped the van with a squeal of brakes. 'What's the matter?' He looked down at Sofia but she was still sound asleep in his wife's arms.

'Over there, look,' said Ana, pointing at a black-and-white painted finger-post sign by the side of the road.

'It's just a sign, what about it?'

'It says "Lower Addenham", yes?' (She pronounced it 'low-vair'.)

'*Lower* Addenham. What about it? It's just a village.'

'Not just a village. I saw in the newspaper and I remember it. It is where *he* is living.'

'He?' said Keir, taking a deep drag on his cigarette and exhaling a stream of smoke upwards. 'Who on earth are you talking about?'

'That *kuzurszh,'* spat Ana.

'I'll have to cover Sofia's ears if you ever say that in English.'

'That one who calls himself king of Fenekslavia, but who is nothing more than a doll of the Austrians.'

'Doll? You mean a puppet, I think.'

'It is all the same. He is an imposter. Drive to this place.'

'Now just a minute old girl,' said Keir, opening the window and flicking his cigarette end out onto the lane, where it fizzled out in a half-frozen puddle. 'Just what are you planning on doing?'

'You will see,' said Ana, looking at him intently. 'Please drive to this Lower Addenham now.'

There was something in Ana's expression, Keir thought, which came from somewhere far, far away from a quiet English country lane; in her eyes he could see a resolve as hard and endless as the Caspian steppe, and in her voice he heard an echo of haunting dulcimer music. Powerless to resist, he crunched the gears once more to turn the van around in the road.

*

'Is that who I think it was?' said Mrs Shaw as she descended the stairs of the vicarage, shortly after Zorard had departed.

'That rather depends upon whom you think it was,' said Shaw, as he opened the door of the dining room for his wife.

'Oh don't tease, Lucian.' You know exactly who I mean. The king of, of, that place.'

'If you are referring to His Majesty King Basil the Second of Fenekslavia, then no, it was not him.'

'Well, one of his servants then. Nobody has a motor car as enormous as that around here, not even Lord Addenham. It looks the sort of thing an American millionaire would own.'

'It is not owned, but hired,' replied Shaw, 'and it was driven by the king's private secretary, Mr Zorard. It seems, my dear, that we do not need to worry about the etiquette of who is to leave cards with whom. I shall be visiting The Larches later this week.'

'You mean you have been summoned?' said Mrs Shaw as they sat down at the dining table. Hettie suddenly appeared behind them without having to be called with the little bell kept on the sideboard for that purpose, and Shaw guessed she had been listening intently from the kitchen door.

'Summoned?' said Shaw. 'You make it sound like I am appearing in a magistrate's court for speeding.'

'You know what I mean. Granted an audience.'

'I don't think it will be anything as impressive as that,'

said Shaw. 'From what I can gather, reading between the lines of what Mr Zorard said, the king is in what are politely termed reduced circumstances. It seems he wishes to live as an ordinary English country gentleman, at least for the time being.'

'How extraordinary. I've never understood these high-ups who act as if they can just become ordinary people.'

Shaw smiled as he tucked into the bacon and eggs placed in front of him by Hettie. 'My dear, surely a high-up becoming an ordinary person is the essence of the Christian religion?'

'Oh that's different, and you know it Lucian, so don't start thinking that's the sort of clever thing to put into your next sermon. And *you* can stop being naughty,' she said to the little terrier, Fraser, as he tried to step up onto her lap.

'It is an interesting theme for a Christmas sermon,' said Shaw. '"Humbled for a season", and so on. A king visited in a stable.'

'I'd hardly call The Larches a stable.'

'Perhaps not. And it would be in poor taste, I think, to make use of one's parishioners for strained analogies in a sermon. Would you pass the toast please?'

'Of course,' said Mrs Shaw. 'But what did he want, this Mr Zorard person?'

'I have been invited to a luncheon and a clay pigeon shoot followed by afternoon tea.'

'What an extraordinary notion. I suppose one has to make allowances for foreigners. But what will you do? You're a hopeless shot. Lord Addenham told you that quite openly when he invited us last time.'

'Only because he compares me with Chaffey, who as far as I can tell was of the now almost extinct breed of hunting parson.'

Shaw pointed to the sepia photograph above the sideboard which showed the previous incumbent, the Reverend Joseph Chaffey DD, with the old Lord Addenham, displaying a brace of pheasants bagged on some shooting party in the long-gone Edwardian era.

'Well it all sounds rather un-clergyman-like to me,' said Mrs Shaw. 'Ought you to be indulging in such aristocratic pleasure?'

'This visit is not merely pleasure,' said Shaw. 'It is also business. It seems the king wishes to be married, and would like to discuss the ceremony. I am to perform a royal wedding.'

Fraser yelped and dashed out of the room as Hettie dropped one of the silver breakfast salvers on the sideboard in shock at what she had just heard.

*

After putting the car away, Zorard closed the doors of the garage a few yards to the side of The Larches, and surveyed his new home. A house neither new nor old, built, according to the inscription on the wall, in 1888. The style was traditional, similar to that he had seen in some parts of Germany, with exposed wooden beams and small leaded windows. It was overshadowed by pine trees and tall hedges which gave it a gloomy, brooding aspect.

He sighed; if only they had had enough money with them to purchase a London house rather than this country-bumpkin place. But then, that was not just because of a lack of money. The king had bought the place on a whim simply because it was close to the theatre in which a certain woman was performing.

Unlike his employer, Zorard had no great love of England or the English. He had spent some time in the country as a young man, where he had picked up the language, but he had always considered it a remote, damp little island, a suet pudding of a country. A land where priests looked and lived like ordinary men, their bland Protestantism bred from long years of comfort and complacency. How different the man Shaw was from the Orthodox priests of Fenekslavia, he thought.

As he walked towards the house he saw King Basil on his morning stroll in the grounds. He looked happy, despite the cold and gloom of the morning.

'Your Majesty,' said Zorard, inclining his head in a low bow. He had decided that the use of the correct title was safe enough in the confines of the house and grounds.

'Ah, good morning, Zorard,' said the king. 'A pretty English winter's morning.' He breathed in the damp air and smiled. 'Refreshing, is it not? The landscape reminds me of my all too brief time at Sandhurst military college. It was there that I perfected my English, of course.'

Zorard merely nodded. He observed the king was wearing a suit of plus-fours, with gaily coloured chequered stockings. As he stood in front of the half-timbered porch of the house, the impression conveyed was not of a king, but of a stockbroker leaving for a round of golf.

'I see His Majesty's new clothes have arrived from London while I was out,' said Zorard.

'Indeed, indeed,' said the king. 'I look quite the English gentleman, no? Huntsman's had my measurements and made them especially quickly without need of seeing me in person. An entire wardrobe. And what is even better, they give long credit. Admirable, do you not think?'

King Basil gave a half turn. 'Most suitable, sir,' said Zorard. He shuddered to think of the cost.

'Let us walk around the grounds a little,' said the king, and the two men strolled slowly along the gravel drive leading to the gate.

'We have some matters to discuss,' said the king. 'You saw the priest? I mean, the vicar?'

'Yes sir. He informs me there are no legal difficulties to your forthcoming marriage and that he will be able to perform the ceremony. He also, after some persuasion, agreed that your adopted English name be used to avoid publicity.'

'Excellent,' said the king. 'And there is no obstruction to marriage of one who is not of his church?'

'It seems not, sir. Under the law of the English anyone resident in the area of the church may be married in it.'

'What a country, Zorard, what a country,' said the king, looking around him with a smile. 'Here a man's religion depends solely on his place of abode.'

The two men had reached the end of the gravel drive where large metal gates barred the way in from the road.

'Keep away from the gates, please, sir,' said Zorard. 'We do not know what lengths the Bolsheviks may go to to take their revenge.'

The king gave a short, loud laugh. 'My dear man. Your concern for the royal person is reassuring, but unnecessary. The newspapers from Kecsprem we requested have arrived via London this morning. In it the Bolsheviks have issued a full pardon.'

The king took a thin newspaper from the inside pocket of his jacket and smoothed it out, then passed it to Zorard, who looked at the article on the front page headed 'Royal Pardon'.

'You see? said the king. 'Those filthy peasants have

graciously consented not to harm me on the understanding that I do not return to my native land.'

Zorard's brow furrowed as he read the full article. 'I do not trust them sir. It could be a Bolshevik trick.'

'You are too cautious, Zorard,' said the king. 'Besides, this is England. Assassins bearing daggers and bombs do not lurk in the hedgerows. Even the policemen do not need to carry revolvers.'

'Nevertheless sir, it would be wise to act as…'

The king cut him off with a raised hand. 'There is no need to worry, Zorard. Now, to the matter in hand – the marriage ceremony.'

The men turned and walked along the drive back to the house.

'With respect, sir, it would be better to wait until your return to Fenekslavia,' said Zorard. 'Then a full royal wedding can be carried out.'

'I know that is your opinion,' said the king, 'but it is not right to keep my intended waiting for a day which will never come.'

'I do not understand, sir. You mean you wish to keep the woman as your mistress?'

'Certainly not,' said the king. 'That is why we procured that cottage for her nearby. It would not be proper for her to be living under my roof before the ceremony. Especially when a priest is to call.'

'But then why should the day never come for a royal wedding in Fenekslavia?' asked Zorard. 'I realise your bride is not…'

'Is not *what*?' said the king, and for the first time Zorard felt he had perhaps overstepped the mark.

'...is not a Fenekslavian,' he added quickly, 'but all the more reason for her to be married in the traditional ceremony in Kecsprem Cathedral. To make her more acceptable to the people. They will also need a spectacle of tradition when you return, once we have defeated the Bolsheviks. Funds and troops are being raised as we speak.'

The king smiled and shook his head slowly. 'My dear, loyal Zorard. I have been thinking much about this these last few days, but I am resolved. The kingdom of Fenekslavia is finished. Most of the royal court have been arrested. The people do not want me. A red tide is creeping across Europe from Moscow, and it is better for us to live out our days in a high place where it cannot reach. That place is England.'

Chapter Three

Alice Burward, the solidly built and grey-haired housekeeper at The Larches, frowned as she watched the butler, Harold Soames, attempting to clean the silver in the kitchen. He was making a proper mess of it, she could see, as if he'd never come across a tin of Silvo and a brush in his life.

With his lean, black-clad figure, lank oily hair and cadaverous expression he looked more like an undertaker polishing coffin handles, she thought. She decided to take a few minutes' break from preparing the luncheon, have a cup of a tea and a look at the latest copy of the *Woman's Weekly*.

'Cup of tea, Mr Soames?' said Mrs Burward, as she filled the kettle.

'No thank you, Mrs Burward,' said Soames, with a nervous laugh. 'I haven't got time to stop, after this I've got to do a sponge and press on His Majesty's tweed suit.'

And that will be another mess, thought Mrs Burward. The last time she had seen him try to use an iron, she had watched him for five minutes before he realised it was stone cold.

All in all it was a rum old do, thought Mrs Burward as she sat down at the big scrubbed oak table in the middle of the kitchen and lit a Craven 'A' cigarette. The old master, Major Chilcot, had been no trouble to look after. He was a bachelor, hardly ever entertained and after a lifetime in the army was almost completely self-sufficient. It had been just like him to die suddenly from a heart attack with no fuss nor bother to anyone, and what's more, with no family to speak of, he'd specified with lawyers that all his furniture, effects and servants went to the next owner.

That was a proper master of the old school, thought Mrs Burward. Not like this new chap. Supposed to be a king, she reflected, but looked more like a music-hall turn with his spats and walking sticks, even once wearing a silk topper in the country. Even the other foreign gentleman, that secretary of his, Mr Zorard, had known that was wrong and had got him to wear a soft hat instead.

To add to it all, this king had claimed he liked English cooking but after two days had started complaining and saying he wished he could taste food from his own country again. Well, thought Mrs Burward, I'm not taking up foreign cooking, or *hot cuisine* as they probably say in his language, at my time of life.

She looked over at Soames, and took a long drag on her cigarette. He was now stabbing the forks into the tin of Silvo and rubbing them around in the wadding. Mr Zorard had said Soames had been sent by some agency which had written to him offering their services. She'd asked Zorard who ran the agency, Charlie Chaplin or Buster Keaton, but the man hadn't got the joke.

She knew it was difficult to get servants these days, and she suspected that the king was not by any means wealthy, but really, Soames was more trouble than he was worth.

One of the little electric bells on the wall buzzed. Mrs Burward looked up and saw the light for 'tradesman's entrance' had lit up on the board which indicated which part of the property required service.

'Who can that be now?' she said, standing up and stubbing out her cigarette in the ashtray. 'I've barely touched my tea.'

'Must be something being delivered,' said Soames. 'I'll go.'

'No, Mr Soames, you stay here please,' said Mrs Burward firmly. 'Tradesman's entrance is answered by me, you answer the front door, as I'm sure you remember.'

'Oh, er, yes of course. Thank you Mrs Burward. Carry on then.'

'I shall, Mr Soames, and as we're of equal standing I'm sure you'll also remember there's no need to give me orders neither.'

Soames merely grunted in reply. The bell rang again and Mrs Burward made her way out through the back door to the gate.

*

Ana pressed the electric bell push by the side gate again. She disliked the idea of servants' entrances and had thought at first to present herself at the front gate, but then decided a little subterfuge was required for what she had in mind. After a minute or so, a buxom, grey-haired lady came out of the house and walked over to the gate.

'Yes, what do you want?' she asked.

'I want to see the king,' said Ana.

'Do you indeed?' said the woman. 'The master of the house is Mr George. I'm sure I don't know any king.'

'I know he is here,' insisted Ana. 'I am not a

newspaper reporter so you do not need to lie.'

'I'll take no moral instruction from you, young lady,' said the woman. 'State your business or be off.'

Ana took out one of the little leaflets advertising the café, that she and Keir carried around to give out to interested parties. She handed it to the woman.

'I am a cook, especially of Fenekslavian dishes. I wish to offer my services to my king.'

'Of all the nerve,' said the woman, but then after a moment's reflection her face brightened a little. 'Fenekslavian dishes, you say?'

'Yes. I am from that country, although my husband is English. We have a small restaurant in Midchester. That is him over there in our van.'

The woman looked across the road to see the small van with 'Midchester Vegetarian Café' painted on the side.

'Hmm,' she said. 'You're a trained cook, are you?'

'Of course,' said Ana, although she neglected to add that her only training had been watching her mother and grandmother at work.

'We are a bit short-handed,' said the woman. 'I suppose I could ask the ki…I mean, Mr George's private secretary to make enquiries.'

'He is a Fenekslavian? I wish to see him.'

'Yes, he's one of you lot. I can't say as he'll see you though. He's had to deal with a few troublemakers from the newspapers already.'

'I do not make trouble and if I speak to him in his native language he will know I am genuine.'

'Well, all right then,' said the woman. 'I dare say it will be in order. It's not as if we stand on ceremony much here anyway. Come this way please.'

The woman opened the gate and Ana walked through, turning to wave briefly to Keir, who tapped at his watch to indicate that she should not be too long. As they walked through the back entrance of the house, the woman turned to Ana.

'By the way, I'm Mrs Burward, the housekeeper. I don't think I caught your name.'

'My name is Ana Walters.'

'Very well Mrs Walters, if you'll kindly wait here I'll see if Mr Zorard is free.'

She gestured for Ana to sit on an upright chair in a long service corridor with green and cream painted walls and a gleaming stone floor. Mrs Burward then knocked on a door a little distance along the corridor; there was a muffled reply and she walked in and closed the door behind her, leaving Ana alone.

Behind the closed door of another room nearby, Ana could hear voices, a man and a woman. From what she could gather they were speaking flirtatiously to one another.

'Oh go on Basil,' said the woman. 'Do let me have a look. I'm dying to know what it feels like as well.'

Ana felt her face flush with embarrassment and she wished that the housekeeper would hurry up and tell her if she was wanted or not. Then she heard the man speak.

'I have already told you my dear, not until we are married.'

'Spoilsport,' teased the woman.

The man then spoke more firmly. ' I have shown you enough. The crown jewels of Fenekslavia must not be worn by its queen until her coronation. Let the ring I gave you previously be sufficient. Let me put the rest away safely.'

There was the sound of a heavy door closing and a key turning in a lock. Then the door to the room opened and, directly in front of Ana, stood a man she recognised immediately as King Basil, despite his English clothes and clean-shaven appearance. Holding onto his arm was a heavily made-up, gaudily-dressed woman with peroxide blonde hair. His mistress, Ana assumed, knowing that Queen Violetta, his wife, had died some years earlier.

Ana stood up and curtseyed deeply before the king, addressing him formally as 'your majesty' in her native language.

King Basil looked at her with a curious gaze, half shocked, half intrigued. He replied to her in Fenekslavian.

'And who are you?'

'My name is Ana Walters, sir.'

'You are a Fenek?'

'Yes sir.'

'And yet your name is of the English.'

'My husband is of the English, sir.'

Ana could see the king's female companion's face bore the look of bored politeness of those unable to understand a conversation in a foreign tongue. King Basil noticed this also and switched to speaking in English.

'What may I do for you Mrs Walters?' he asked. 'Oh, by the way, may I present my intended, Miss Elsie Garnham.'

The peroxide blonde woman nodded coldly at Ana. She had seen that look before. The English women of that type often seemed to be angered by her, she noticed; she suspected they were jealous of her looks and natural slim figure.

Ana curtseyed to Elsie, rather less grandly than she had to the king.

'Your majesty,' said Ana, 'I heard of your arrival and wished to be of service to my country…that is, my country of birth, to offer my services as a cook to His Majesty.'

'You should be speaking to the housekeeper, not His

Majesty,' said Elsie coldly. 'I assume it was her that let you in but I don't know why she's left you to wander the corridors.'

'Forgive me madam...' protested Ana, and at that moment Mrs Burward appeared.

'I'm ever so sorry sir,' said Mrs Burward. 'I was speaking to Mr Zorard about this young woman. She's applied for the position of cook.'

'So I have established, Mrs Burward, said King Basil. 'Perhaps you would allow me to question her myself.'

Mrs Burward made a sort of awkward bob. 'Of course sir. Only Mr Zorard has just told me he doesn't want us to take on any more staff.'

'Yes, yes,' said the king, dismissively. 'Zorard is always holding the wallet strings tightly, as the English say. I, however, still believe in the concept of *noblesse oblige*, as the French say.'

'I don't quite follow, sir,' said Mrs Burward.

King Basil looked upwards for inspiration then spoke. 'The English poet Hilaire Belloc puts it thus: "It is the duty of the wealthy man, to give employment to the artisan."'

'Very good, sir,' said Mrs Burward, who looked as if she had no idea what the king was talking about. 'But saving your presence, you'll allow me to remain so that I can show the young woman out when you've finished.'

'Quite so, quite so,' said the king, and Mrs Burward retreated a few feet to stand watching them, with her hands clasped in front of her.

'Now then,' said the king to Ana. 'You are able to cook Fenekslavian dishes?'

'Of course, sir.'

'Such as *šémecška* in the Kecsprem style, and *kérekměves* cutlets, the boiled kind as well as the fried?'

'Naturally,' replied Ana with a smile. 'And desserts

also. What the English call pudding.'

'Oh…' said the king with an exhalation of breath. 'I have only been here a short while, but my word, how I miss *gómloi żamuska* puddings.'

'The type with the cream is my speciality.'

Ana looked at the king and saw he was almost drooling. The woman, Elsie, was looking daggers at her. She smiled inwardly. So much the better if her presence caused upset in the king's love affairs. The stupid sensual fool had fallen for her, she was sure.

'*Veclevarcept*', said the king, clapping his hands together. 'Or, to put it in English, it is done. You will begin straight away.'

'I have a family and a business of my own to run, sir,' replied Ana. 'I am only able to work at certain times.'

'As you wish,' said the king. 'Mrs Burward will make the arrangements of pay and hours and so on.'

Mrs Burward nodded, but was pushed out of the way by a man who rushed out of one of the doors on to the corridor. Ana assumed this must be Zorard.

'Sir, forgive me for this intrusion,' said the man. 'I expressly told Mrs Burward we did not require any more domestic staff.' He turned to Ana and addressed her sharply.

'Young lady, you may go.'

Ana looked to the king, who waved his hand at Zorard.

'Too late, Zorard, too late. I have already engaged the young lady as a part-time cook.'

Zorard sighed. 'As you wish, sir. But I trust you will allow me to check this lady's references? We know nothing of her, and…'

'And you believe she may be a Bolshevik spy sent to poison me,' said the king with a laugh. 'My dear Zorard, as I said before, we are in England, not a melodrama of the Kecsprem Opera. Spies do not lurk here.'

Zorard turned, with a look of slight embarrassment, away from Ana and lowered his voice in a pointless attempt to make himself less easily heard.

'I had no intention to impute the young lady's character, sir. I am merely being careful.'

'I did not rule a nation without being able to judge character,' replied the king, 'and I judge this young lady to be of positive benefit to this household. Mrs Burward, kindly take Mrs Walters to the kitchen and show her around.'

*

A few days later, Shaw arrived at The Larches shortly before luncheon. The pretty snowfall of the previous days had largely melted away; slush coated the road and so he had had to keep his speed down on his bicycle to avoid mishaps; but Shaw, who did not own a motor car, was used to bicycling in all sorts and conditions of weather.

All morning he had noticed a hymn tune going round in his head. In his experience this usually meant something; but for the present he could not work out what it could be. It was *All My Hope on God is Founded*, a modern composition, by the poet Robert Bridges, although Shaw thought it was perhaps based on some earlier text.

He hummed the tune, again a modern one. It was by Herbert Howells, as far as he could recall; the organist at All Saints tended to keep abreast of musical developments and so Shaw was used to hearing both ancient and modern hymnody.

What could it mean? Inspiration, he decided, was best not forced, but allowed to come in God's good time.

The only thing about this parish visit he was not quite sure about was clothing; normally he would have worn his dark suit for a professional visit, but as this also included a clay pigeon shoot, he decided on tweeds with a dog collar. He reflected that the 'hunting parsons' of the eighteenth century had not had this problem, since the clerical collar had not been the norm for clergy until about 80 years previously.

Zorard met Shaw at the gate and the butler wheeled Shaw's bicycle away to the garage. In the hallway Shaw handed his hat, coat and heavy muffler to Mrs Burward, whom he vaguely recognised and with whom he exchanged pleasantries about the weather.

They traversed a corridor decorated with pieces of ancient tarnished armour, and oil paintings so darkened by age that it was impossible to make out their subjects. Zorard then took Shaw into the gloomy panelled dining room where a sleek, well-groomed man and a rather overdressed woman stood up to greet him.

'Your majesty,' said Zorard, bowing from the waist. 'May I present the Reverend Mr Shaw of All Saints' church.'

Shaw stepped forward and bowed briefly from the neck.

'Your majesty.'

'My dear vicar,' replied the king, 'how good to finally meet you.' Shaw noticed he already had a half-empty glass of wine in his hand.

'This is my fiancée, Miss Elsie Garnham.'

Elsie merely nodded at Shaw, flashed him a brittle smile and uttered a curt 'how do you do,' to which Shaw responded in kind.

'Now, let us eat, and discuss the happy day,' said the king, ringing a small bell on the table.

The group sat at one end of the large Jacobean dining table (a replica, thought Shaw, though he could not be certain). The king and Elsie sat at one end, with Shaw and Zorard at right angles facing each other. Mrs Burward, the butler, and another servant of some sort, a young woman, entered the room and the king asked them to serve luncheon.

'The vicar will of course give a blessing first,' said King Basil.

Shaw stood and spoke the brief Latin grace he had used since his college days:

'Benedictus benedicat, per Jesum Christum Dominum nostrum. Amen.'

'Splendid, splendid,' said the king. 'It is right that an English gentleman should have such a priest to his lunch table, no?'

Shaw wondered who the 'English gentleman' was. He caught a look of distaste from both Zorard and Elsie and realised that the king must be referring to himself. He could not help feeling rather like a stage-clergyman, called on to play a part in a rich man's aristocratic fancies.

'The meal will be a mixture of English and Fenekslavian cuisine, Mr Shaw,' said the king. 'My new cook, Mrs Ana Walters, is one of my compatriots, and has produced courses for all tastes. You will find the meal delightful, I hope.'

'Wait,' said Zorard. 'If your majesty will permit, I ask the food to be tasted first.'

'My dear Zorard,' said the king. 'We have no royal taster here, and besides, I do not think we need one. You will make Mr Shaw nervous.'

'With your majesty's permission, a brief test.'

'Very well, proceed, Zorard,' said the king. 'But hurry, I am hungry.'

'Not I sir,' replied Zorard. He turned to the corner of the room and addressed the young woman servant. 'Mrs Walters, please taste the dishes that you have put on the sideboard.'

Shaw noticed a flash of anger cross the face of Ana, but it was quickly replaced by a bland politeness. She ate a small portion of each of the dishes laid out, then turned to the king.

'As you can see, sir, I am still alive,' said Ana, her voice tinged with sarcasm.

'You will not address His Majesty in such a way,' snapped Zorard.

'Come, come Zorard,' said the king. 'The ritual has been performed. Mrs Walters remains alive. Let us eat! You will pardon the formality, Mr Shaw. A precaution from my days in a country where I had many enemies.'

'I quite understand,' said Shaw, although he could not help wondering just what on earth he was getting himself into.

Shaw could not help also noticing during the meal that the butler seemed remarkably inept; not only did he fumble and drop cutlery once or twice but he also served a dessert wine with the first course, and some sort of sherry, as far as Shaw could make out, with the main course. Neither the king, Elsie nor Zorard seemed to notice. Shaw did not mind himself particularly, knowing there was a servant shortage, but it seemed odd that even a king did not seem able to find someone competent.

The Fenekslavian food was excellent, reflected Shaw, and actually did not go too badly with the sweet sherry served by the butler, so perhaps, he thought, it was an intentional choice after all. He began to relax slightly despite the rather stilted and formal conversation around the table.

'To business, then,' said the king after they had finished eating. He wiped his mouth with the napkin he had spread out across his shirt-front. 'Although I trust there will not be much business, as a small wedding in a country church will not require much planning.'

'What do you mean, small wedding?' said Elsie, who hitherto had not really said anything at all. 'You said we were going to be married in a big royal wedding. In a cathedral.'

Shaw suddenly felt an atmosphere in the room, and noticed that Elsie was breathing hard. The king placed his hand on hers but she snatched it away.

'My dear,' said the king, smoothly, 'perhaps I should have mentioned it before, but matters have arisen which make it highly unlikely that I will return to Fenekslavia in the foreseeable future. But rest assured, you will still be my queen, even if in exile.'

Elsie appeared to struggle to maintain her composure. She took a deep breath. 'I suppose that will have to do then.'

It was not the first time, Shaw reflected, that a couple that seemed somewhat unsuited had come to him to discuss marriage, but the previous cases had all been youngsters who had indulged in forbidden passions, and who had had no choice but to marry when the inevitable occurred.

He sighed inwardly. He had no right to refuse anyone the sacrament of marriage, except for strictly legal reasons. He hoped however, that he might be able to counsel them to reflect on their best course of action.

After luncheon and some brief discussion of the practicalities of organising a church wedding, the small party of four made their way out onto the little patch of land to the rear of The Larches; part garden, part unused pasture. Snow had begun to fall, and the low sun dappled the ground with orange light when it occasionally appeared. It was not an ideal setting for a shoot, thought Shaw, but he indulged the king's desire to offer what he presumably thought was traditional English hospitality.

Soames, the butler, staggered behind them under the weight of several guns and bags of cartridges that he had brought out from the house, while Zorard set up a folding table and various other paraphernalia.

'Of course,' said King Basil, 'in my homeland we had many estate workers to organise shoots. Here we must make shift with clay pigeons and Mr Zorard, who served in the Engineers before he became my equerry. Have the new equipment and guns all arrived from London?'

'They have, majesty,' said Zorard. 'At great expense from Holland and Holland, just as you asked.'

'Good, good,' said the king. 'Mr Shaw, you will please choose your weapon.' The king gestured to the firearms which Soames, breathing heavily, had laid out on the folding table.

Shaw glanced at the table and selected a shotgun.

'Come come, Mr Shaw,' said the king, with amusement. 'That is a 28-bore. A lady's gun!'

'A 28-bore will be quite sufficient for clays,' said Shaw. 'I would rather avoid a bruised shoulder. It may impede my ability to administer Holy Communion this Sunday.'

The king laughed. 'As you wish. Now, you may have the first shot, as our guest.'

Zorard pointed to a clump of trees at the end of the garden. 'The trap is there. The, what is the word, the trajectory, is between the trees. Ready?'

Shaw nodded, loaded his gun and stepped forward.

He raised the weapon to his shoulder and shouted 'Pull!'

A clay shot across the sky before he had even uttered the order, and he fired; he chipped the disk very slightly and it landed intact somewhere on the other side of the garden.

'Bad luck, Mr Shaw,' said the king. Try again.'

Shaw opened his mouth to shout, but Zorard placed a hand on his arm. 'There is no need to shout, Mr Shaw,' he said.

'But how will the boy hear?' asked Shaw in confusion.

Zorard laughed. 'There is no boy operating the trap,' he said. 'This is the latest device, from London. It is controlled by cable, and a dry cell battery. Look, I operate the trap remotely from this switch.' Shaw looked down and saw that Zorard held a small box in his hand, with a cable attached which snaked away to the bottom of the garden.

'Ingenious,' said Shaw. 'A pity though; the local boys have been deprived of their shillings for the work.'

Zorard smiled politely. 'The fewer outsiders we have here, the better, I think,' he said. 'Ready?'

Shaw nodded, and Zorard pressed a button on the box in his hand. The trap sprung and the disk flew across the sky. This time, Shaw was ready for it, and tracked its progress with the gun barrel, then fired. The disk exploded in a satisfying burst of ceramic fragments.

'Good shot sir!' shouted the king. 'Now, my dear, your turn.'

Elsie turned to the table and looked at the guns. 'Here,' she said, pointing at one of them, 'what's this thing doing here? That's a hunting rifle.'

Zorard looked at the table. 'Idiot,' he said to Soames, who was standing by the table. The butler flinched visibly. 'That is not one of the guns that arrived from London. It is one of the previous owners, that was sold with the house. Take it back. Do you not know the difference between a hunting rifle and a shotgun?'

'Very sorry, sir,' said Soames, and picked up the rifle.

'Wait,' said King Basil. 'This is a chance for you to show off your skill, my dear.'

'What do you mean?' said Elsie.

'Mr Shaw perhaps does not know you are a performer in the theatre, with shooting as your speciality.'

'Indeed, I was not aware of that,' said Shaw. 'Most interesting.'

'Most women I have known,' said the king with a smile, 'have struggled to shoot a clay even with a shotgun. I wager my Elsie could do it with a rifle.'

'Oh don't bang on, Basil,' said Elsie. 'I'm not a blasted performing seal.'

'Perhaps you are not able to,' teased the king.

'Don't be so bloo…so silly,' said Elsie. She took the rifle from Soames, adjusted the sights and worked the bolt, quickly establishing that it was loaded, then raised it to her shoulder.

'Pull,' she said laconically, nodding at Zorard.

There was the sound of the trap being sprung and the clay came into view for a split second before there was a loud bang and it shattered into pieces. With a bored expression Elsie worked back the bolt, ejecting the spent cartridge onto the ground. She handed the rifle back to Soames.

'Satisfied?' she said to the king.

'Marvellous, marvellous,' said King Basil, who had watched the feat with an expression of awe.

*

By four pm the midwinter sun had set and the small group made its way back to the house. A light snowfall had begun and Shaw's boots creaked on the crisp, even powder on the ground. He was looking forward to a warming drink before the cold bicycle ride home. The shoot had gone on a little too long for his liking, with the king keen to show off his prowess with his new, expensive 'over under' shotgun.

Once inside the drawing room, where the curtains were already drawn and a fire blazed in the grate, Shaw began to thaw out. After Soames, and later Zorard, had arrived back from putting the guns away, tea was served. Again, Shaw noticed that Soames did not seem to quite know what he was doing. He had used a silver coffee pot for the tea which imparted a strange taste to the brew.

Mrs Burward must have noticed because Shaw heard her say 'Would you kindly fetch some more tea, Mr Soames, in the teapot this time.' Soames backed out of the room in embarrassed silence.

'A splendid shoot, eh, Mr Shaw?' said the king, jovially. 'Worthy of the great English estates, no doubt?' He squeezed Elsie's waist.

Shaw considered mentioning that clay shooting was really only a practice activity for a proper game shoot, but decided not to disappoint the king.

'Your majesty shoots well,' he said instead. 'I am sure you will be a welcome guest with any of the large landowners of the county.'

'Perhaps, ' said the king. 'But I will take with me my secret weapon. That will be the real attraction.'

'Secret...weapon?' asked Shaw.

'My bride, of course!' said the king, squeezing Elsie even harder. 'The Annie Oakley of England! She will kill more pheasants than anyone! The landowners will invite us regularly to see her shoot, I am sure.'

Again, Shaw did not want to disappoint the king by mentioning that the aristocracy of Suffolk might look somewhat askance at a music-hall sharpshooter despatching their game stocks with perfect precision. He need not have worried, as Elsie spoke out angrily.

'I thought I was going to be giving up all that,' she said. 'When I become queen it wouldn't be right.'

'Right?' said the king. 'Of course, it will be right. You are a joy to watch in action. In fact, I no longer even wish you to end your stage career. It was watching you on stage in Kecsprem that made me first fall in love with you. Each time I travel to the music-hall I shall fall in love with you all over again. That is the main reason I moved to this place, to be nearer to you, rather than stay in London.'

Elsie's jaw dropped. 'You mean you want me to go back to that...well of all the...first no royal wedding, now I'm supposed to go back on the stage after telling everyone I was leaving? Sounds like I'll be no more royal than a pearly queen in the East End of London!'

With that, Elsie stood up and stormed out of the room, slamming the door behind her.

'My dear Shaw, I am so sorry,' said the king, with a puzzled expression on his face. 'Did I say something wrong? What is a "pearly queen"?'

Shaw sighed inwardly, and suppressed a selfish wish that he had never become involved in this. He was now duty bound, he felt, to organise some sort of pre-wedding discussion about the problems between the two.

'I am sorry, Mr Shaw,' began the king. Before he could

continue, Zorard leapt to his feet.

'Quiet,' he snapped, then turned his head to one side, as if listening for something.

'Zorard, what is it…?' said the king.

'Your majesty, please, quiet,' said Zorard. He then walked quickly to the window, and drew aside the curtain slightly. He raised the sash and listened closely at the gap, pressing his body against the wall beside the window.

'Zorard, what is happening, please explain,' said the king, angrily.

'One moment sir,' said Zorard. 'Everybody remain calm and still.'

'There is somebody outside the window!' shouted Zorard, leaping back. There was then a loud crash as an object shattered the window and landed with a thud on the carpet.

'A rock!' shouted the king. 'Who dares throw…'

'Your majesty, quiet please!' ordered Zorard. He strode to the door and switched off the lights. 'Everybody remain exactly where they are.'

The room was plunged into absolute darkness, but for a moment, the moon appeared from behind the clouds and Shaw glimpsed the pristine whiteness of the freshly snow-covered courtyard through the window, then the lunar light disappeared and all was dark again.

An instant later, there was a flash of light and a deafening explosion from the direction of the window. Instinct, and his time in the trenches as a military chaplain took over, and he flung himself to the floor.

'I see him!' shouted Zorard from the direction of the window. 'He has run away!' The room was then bathed in a dim light as he turned on a small table lamp. 'Everybody, keep down,' he ordered.

Shaw looked around the room, and noticed that the

king appeared nowhere to be seen. Mrs Burward was standing by the sofa, looking down and whimpering. Shaw crossed the room to her, crouching low.

'Oh sir,' she said, holding her hand to her mouth. 'I think he's dead, sir.'

Zorard also crossed the room from the window, and looked down. Shaw knelt. He had seen enough death in the war to know that the king, lying on the carpet, was mortally wounded. His shirt-front was soaked in blood and he clutched at the area of his heart. His eyes stared fixedly ahead and his breathing came in low, shallow gasps.

'Mrs Burward, get help immediately,' said Shaw. 'Telephone to Dr Ellis. His number is Netley 391.'

Mrs Burward appeared frozen to the spot. 'Mrs Burward, now!' said Shaw firmly, and the woman appeared to regain her composure. She rushed into the corridor and Shaw heard her running towards the telephone in the hallway.

'It is too late, I fear,' said Zorard.

A low whisper came from the king's lips and he held Shaw's arm with a weak grip.

'Forgive…me.'

Shaw nodded. He took the king's hand and recited what he could remember of the Order for the Visitation of the Sick in the Prayer Book. He began haltingly but then with assurance as the words came to him clearly.

'Our Lord Jesus Christ, who hath left…who hath left power to his church to forgive…to *absolve* all sinners who truly repent and believe in him, of his great mercy forgive thee thine offences: and by his authority committed to me, I absolve thee from all thy sins, in the name of the Father, and of the Son, and of the Holy Ghost. Amen.'

Shaw made the sign of the cross and felt the king's

grip loosen; the remaining colour drained from his face and his skin took on a waxy sheen, as if an invisible hand had passed over it, removing the life-force as it went.

Shaw pressed down on the man's eyelids for a few seconds, and once he was sure they were closed, he lifted his hand. He reached for the linen cloth on the tea-table and lowered it over the king's face.,

Zorard's heels clicked loudly together as he stood to attention and pronounced something formal-sounding in what Shaw assumed was Fenekslavian. For Shaw's benefit, he repeated it in English.

'The king is dead. Long live the king!'

Chapter Four

Once he realised that no more could be done for the king, Shaw suddenly remembered the rock that had been thrown through the window. Crouching low, he scanned the room and saw that it had fallen on the Turkish carpet near the fire.

As he looked more closely he saw that what had first appeared a rock seemed to be a lump of paper.

'Mr Zorard,' he whispered. 'That object thrown through the window. What is it?'

Zorard's gaze followed Shaw's pointing finger. 'A rock,' he said, 'thrown presumably to break the window and allow a better shot from outside.'

'It's covered with paper,' said Shaw.

Gingerly he picked up the heavy stone, about the size of a cricket ball, and placed it on the tea table. It was a rock covered with a sheet of crumpled paper. Shaw opened it and saw, printed in heavy capitals, a sentence in what he assumed was Fenekslavian. Below it was written in English:

THE HOUSE IS SURROUNDED.
DO NOT ATTEMPT TO LEAVE.
PLACE THE CROWN JEWELS BY THE FRONT

DOOR WITHIN ONE HOUR.
DO NOT ATTEMPT TO GET HELP
OR LEAVE THE HOUSE UNTIL DAWN
OR MORE WILL DIE.
LONG LIVE THE REVOLUTION!

Shaw handed the note silently to Zorard, who scanned it and then put it in his jacket pocket.

'It is as I thought,' he said. 'The Bolsheviks have taken their revenge. I begged and begged the king to allow the British police to protect him but he would not listen.'

'We must get help,' said Shaw. 'But first, where are Miss Garnham and the servants?'

Before Zorard had a chance to answer, the housekeeper rushed into the room, almost colliding with the two men inside.

'Oh sir,' said Mrs Burward. 'Is he…' She stopped speaking as she looked down at the body on the floor.

'Yes, Mrs Burward,' said Shaw. 'It appears someone outside shot the king through the window. Please stay in the corridor – we must all stay out of sight.'

Ana appeared behind Mrs Burward; she saw the body on the floor and gasped.

'Please go back and telephone again, for the police this time Mrs Burward,' said Shaw. 'I will accompany you. Where is Miss Garnham, please?'

'I don't know where she is sir, I didn't see her on the way to the telephone,' said Mrs Burward, anxiously. 'And it didn't work not a bit, anyway. The thing's gone dead. I tried rattling the little bar on the top, like they do in the pictures, but it didn't do no good.'

'It is likely the telephone lines have been cut,' said Zorard. 'I will check. All stay with me, and stay away from the windows. Mr Shaw, will you please take up the rear?'

'Where is the butler?' said Ana. 'What if…'

Zorard cut her off. 'Silence. Stay quiet and keep your theories to yourself. You are as much one to be watched as him, as you were out of the room when the king was shot.'

Ana's eyes flashed fire. 'You dare accuse me of…'

'Mrs Walters,' said Shaw firmly, 'let us all keep our heads. We may be in very grave danger. Please remain calm and stay with us as we check the telephone.'

Ana nodded reluctantly and Shaw ushered her into the corridor. Zorard took a poker from beside the fire as he led the way into the hall. Before he left the room, Shaw seized the small shovel from the coal bucket, then walked behind Ana and Mrs Burward, half turning to watch behind. He wondered just how much protection a small metal shovel would give against a gunman.

The little group reached the telephone in the hall. Zorard picked up the receiver and then replaced it.

'Dead,' he said, then walked to the front door. He checked it was locked, and then glanced carefully through one of the windows on the side of the door, onto the illuminated porch.

'The line has been cut,' he said. 'See, Mr Shaw, on the wall there.'

Shaw kept close to the wall and glanced through the window from over Zorard's shoulder. He noticed a neatly cut piece of cable hanging down from the brickwork.

'Oh Lord,' said Mrs Burward. 'You mean whoever killed the king did that and all? That means we can't call the police.'

'I am afraid so, Mrs Burward,' said Shaw. 'The object thrown through the window before the king was shot was a rock with a note tied to it. A person or persons unknown is demanding the crown jewels of Fenekslavia be handed over.'

'If they had not been taken from my country in the first place this would not have happened,' said Ana, angrily.

'I said silence!' said Zorard. 'The crown jewels were taken to prevent them being stolen and sold by the Bolsheviks. It seems they are still trying to steal them and I for one am prepared to die to prevent that. Are you?'

Ana breathed deeply and nodded. 'I am prepared. But for myself only. Innocent people should not die to protect the symbol of a nation not their own.'

Shaw could see an argument was brewing, and attempted to calm the situation. 'Please let us remain calm. We have one hour, almost, to hand over the crown jewels. Mr Zorard, I presume you do have access to them?'

'They are in His Majesty's office. I have the keys.'

'Very well. Then I suggest that one of us must try to get help as quickly as possible, in order that those outside – whoever they are – can be apprehended as they attempt to leave the grounds with the jewels. There is a telephone in the lane about half a mile away – I will endeavour to get to it and summon assistance.'

'Do not be insane,' hissed Zorard. 'You are unarmed. If they see you, they could shoot you down like one of those clay pigeons.'

Mrs Burward swallowed hard and spoke up. 'There's another way, sir,' she said. 'I've just remembered, there's another telephone in the garage.'

Zorard turned to her. 'That will not work either if the line is cut.'

'It's a different line, I think,' said Mrs Burward. 'I remember Major Chilcot had it put in when we had a driver living in the little flat above. Had a different number anyway, Addenham 412, and the house is 455.'

'Good thinking, Mrs Burward,' said Shaw. 'It may still

work. It will be easier for me to get to the garage than all the way to the lane.'

'Preposterous,' said Zorard. 'I will not allow a priest to take such an action. I will go.'

Before Shaw could protest, Zorard walked to the door. 'Everybody, stay out of the way,' he said. 'Keep back from the door, in the side corridors. If I am not back in ten minutes, please assume that I have been shot. Mr Shaw, you must then take over.'

'Very well,' said Shaw, ushering Ana and Mrs Burward into the corridor, away from the main hallway.

'Keep well back,' said Zorard.

Shaw and the ladies kept their backs to the wall of the side corridor. Shaw listened intently as he heard the latch click on the front door and felt a blast of cold air blow through the corridor.

'You scoundrel!' he heard Zorard shout; then two shots rang out and the door slammed; there were sounds of heavy, rapid footfalls on the stone floor of the hallway.

Shaw gestured for Ana and Mrs Burward to move behind him, and then raised the coal shovel high above his head. A figure appeared in the corridor and Shaw breathed a sigh of relief as he saw it was Zorard.

'It is not possible to get to the garage from there,' said Zorard, breathing heavily. 'A man, or possibly two, fired at me.'

'Are you hurt?' enquired Shaw.

'No, no, I am well,' said Zorard. 'I will try the back door. It is possible they do not have enough men to watch that also.'

Zorard walked swiftly along the service corridor which lead to the kitchens and the back door. Shaw and the ladies kept close behind him. Once Zorard had arrived at the back door, he motioned for them to keep back.

He opened the door slowly and then opened it sufficiently to allow room for him to squeeze through.

Those watching him held their breath as he disappeared from view. Shaw's heart skipped a beat as another shot rang out. Moments later Zorard leapt back into the corridor and slammed the door shut, ramming the bolts home.

He gestured for the group to move back into the hallway. Once there, he shook his head, mopping his perspiring brow with his handkerchief.

'The fiends are watching the back of the house also,' he said, angrily. 'I saw them in the bushes. We dare not risk going outside again.'

'Very well,' said Shaw. 'For the moment, we must consider another course of action. We still do not know where Miss Garnham and the butler are. They could be lying hurt somewhere.'

'Of course, of course, you are right, Mr Shaw,' said Zorard. 'We must look for them.'

'Begging your pardon sir,' said Mrs Burward in a quavering voice to Zorard, 'only something's just occurred to me. That back door was locked by me before I come up to serve the tea things. I always bolt it at nightfall. Yet when you went outside it was unlocked.'

'Of what importance is this?' asked Zorard.

Mrs Burward seemed unable to speak.

'I think what Mrs Burward is suggesting,' said Shaw, 'that whoever hostile force is outside, may also be *inside* the house.'

'And it is also possible,' said Ana, glancing around her with a steely gaze, 'that somebody inside the house let them in.'

*

In the back room of a government office in Fenekslavia's capital, several men, some of them in military uniform, were gathered around a table covered with various types of radio sets, Morse code transceivers and headsets.

The men sat or stood in a pool of light from a small table lamp, the only source of illumination in the room. An armed guard with a Thomson gun slung across his front stood impassively by the door, his gaze seemingly hypnotised by the sight of endless snowflakes drifting past the large plate-glass French windows on the opposite side of the room.

A young man wearing a telephonist's headset was rapidly writing on a pad, as the sounds of static whistling from radio equipment rose and fell. He tore off a page from the pad and handed it to a tall, unshaven man in military uniform, who read the transcription slowly.

'Comrades,' announced the man to those around him. 'Our agents in England have placed a telephone call to the Russian embassy in London, and our comrades there have kindly relayed the message to us via their long-range coded radio. I am pleased to tell you that the plan has gone into operation.'

There was a moment of silence as the men looked at each other. Then one older man, with a clear voice, began intoning the words of a Fenekslavian revolutionary song.

He stamped his boot on the floor to the beat, which gradually became faster as the others joined in with the singing. Before long, the singing reached fever pitch and the men clasped each other on the back and began dancing in a circle round the table. The young technician seated at the radio tried vainly at first to protect his equipment, but then gave up and joined in with the exultant singing and dancing.

*

'Miss Garnham! Soames! Where are you? Show yourselves!' Zorard shouted as he led the little group of Ana, Mrs Burward and Shaw along the dimly lit corridor back to the drawing room.

'I'm here.' Elsie appeared further along the corridor. She looked at Zorard with a shocked expression.

'What's going on?' she asked. 'I was sitting in the billiard room trying to…trying to compose myself, and then I heard glass breaking and shots – I kept out of sight and tried to find the rest of you but couldn't.'

'I am afraid we have some bad news, Miss Garnham,' said Shaw, stepping forward next to Zorard. 'The king has been shot, we believe by assassins.'

A look of horror crossed Elsie's face. 'But he said nobody would dare, that the Bolshies had pardoned him, or something.'

'It seems not,' said Shaw.

'Is he…?'

'I regret to inform you he is dead, Miss Garnham,' said Shaw, taking both the woman's hands in his. Her skin was cold to the touch and her hands trembled.

'I don't believe it,' she gasped, and ran to the door of the drawing room.

'Miss Garnham, please…' said Shaw, but it was too late. The little group followed her into the room and found her crouched by the body of King Basil, replacing the linen cloth over his face.

'It happened very quickly,' said Shaw, crouching beside her, 'and he could not have felt much pain.'

Elsie took a deep breath and they both stood up. Shaw sensed she was a strong character, and was hiding the shock well, or perhaps…he dismissed the thought and concentrated on the matter in hand.

'But why are we all just standing here?' said Elsie, her voice rising with panic. 'Why haven't the police been called, or a doctor?'

'There, there, madam,' said Mrs Burward, putting her arm around Elsie. 'We've all got to keep our heads.'

'Please come out of this room, it is not safe,' said Zorard, herding the group back out into the corridor.

'Mr Zorard is right,' said Shaw. 'We have reason to believe that agents of a foreign power are outside the house. They threw a note through the window.'

Zorard took out the note from his pocket, smoothed it out and showed it to Elsie. She read the note quickly and thrust it back into Zorard's hand.

'And we're just standing around here while those ba…those people outside are waiting to rob and kill us?' she said angrily.

'What else do you suggest?' said Zorard. 'The telephones are cut. I was shot several times when I attempted to leave the house.'

'We've got a room full of shotguns and a hunting rifle here,' said Elsie. 'We could shoot our way out. Better than sitting her waiting like sitting ducks.'

She looked around her. 'Where's Soames?'

'We do not know,' said Ana. 'It is my belief he may be one of the criminals.'

'So might you be,' snapped Zorard.

'This is not the time for accusations,' interrupted Shaw firmly. It was highly dangerous, he thought, for the group to turn on one another when they needed to work together.

'We still have not found Soames,' said Shaw. 'He could be lying injured somewhere. We do not know, either, if the house has been infiltrated by the assassins. Miss Garnham is right; we have a room full of guns and we may be able to affect an escape using them, but only as a last resort. Mr Zorard, I suggest we arm ourselves and then search the house thoroughly, then decide how best to proceed. '

'Of course,' said Zorard. 'First, we must lock this door.' He turned to the drawing room door behind him. 'The window is broken and could be used to gain entry. Mrs Burward, do you have the key, please?'

'Yes sir,' said Mrs Burward, taking a large bunch of keys from her apron pocket. She selected one but hesitated before putting it into the lock.

'It don't seem right somehow for the master to be left lying there on the floor…' she said.

'Mrs Burward,' insisted Zorard, 'there is no time for sentimentality. There are people outside, and possibly inside, who are prepared to kill us to get what they want. Kindly lock the door and then we will proceed to search the house.'

'Very good sir,' said Mrs Burward, turning the key in the lock.

'Now, follow me to the gun room, and stay close together,' said Zorard.

The group made its way down the corridor, moving as quietly as possible as each person strained his or her ears and eyes for any unusual sound or movement in the nooks and crannies of the darkened house. Zorard carefully opened each door along the way, and once he was satisfied the rooms were empty, Mrs Burward locked them. Eventually the group reached a door at the end of the corridor.

'That's the gun room,' said Elsie. 'I'll feel a lot safer once I've got a twelve-bore in my hands.'

Zorard stepped forward and reached for the handle.

'Wait,' hissed Shaw.

'What is it?' said Zorard, half turning.

'Look,' whispered the clergyman. He pointed out of the corridor window. The courtyard outside was just visible in the moonlight which reflected off the layers of snow on the ground. Also visible was the window of the room they were about to enter; it was broken.

'That room is opposite the drawing room,' said Shaw. 'I noticed it earlier when I looked out. Both windows are broken, which suggests that whoever shot the king…'

'Did it from the gun room,' said Zorard.

'Possibly,' said Shaw, 'and may even still be inside.'

'Please stand back, everybody,' whispered Zorard, raising his poker. 'Mr Shaw, take the women back to that alcove by the stairs. If I do not emerge from the room, you must get upstairs and lock yourselves in one of the bedrooms.'

Shaw nodded, wondering just exactly how he was going to defend the group against armed assassins with only a shovel. The Lord will provide, he said to himself, as he ushered the women back to the alcove. From there they watched Zorard turn the handle of the gun room door with agonising slowness.

Zorard flung open the door and leapt inside; there was the sound of heavy objects, furniture perhaps, being overturned, and moments later he emerged from the room.

'The room is empty,' he said, breathing slightly

heavily. 'I checked everywhere. But come, Mr Shaw, see what I have found.'

Shaw and the three women crowded through the door. The gun room, lit only by a dim bulb, was filled with the usual paraphernalia of such places, most of it, Shaw assumed, the property of the late Major Chilcot which had been sold with the house. Fishing rods, nets, mackintoshes, tweed hats and wellington boots hung from the walls or lay on chairs and tables; in the corner was a pile of some sort of machinery and electrical cables, largely concealed under grey blankets. An icy breeze blew through a broken pane in the window.

'The gun cabinet has been left open,' said Zorard, pointing to a tall, dark wooden cupboard by the door. In it could be seen a row of neatly stacked shotguns. 'I told Soames to ensure he locked it after replacing the weapons this afternoon.'

'And we still don't know where he is,' said Elsie. 'Ten to one he's in on it.'

'We should not just stand around talking,' said Ana. 'We should take the guns and get help.'

'Even if it were your place to make such a suggestion,' said Zorard icily to Ana, 'there would be no point. I see that the cartridges have been taken. I ordered several hundred from Holland and Holland and placed them in the cabinet myself, but they have all gone.'

'So we've got a brace of shotguns but nothing to put in them,' said Elsie. She strode to the cabinet, took out the guns and broke them open. 'All empty. About as much use as a chocolate teapot.'

'What is a chocolate teapot?' asked Ana, with a puzzled expression on her face.

'It's just a saying, dear,' said Elsie with a sigh. 'I mean we'll have to give up the idea of shooting our way out.'

'It would have been an extremely dangerous thing to do, anyway,' said Shaw. 'Getting away quietly, under the cover of darkness, is our best hope.'

'There is something else,' said Zorard. 'I found this on the floor.' He bent down and picked up the hunting rifle with which Elsie had demonstrated her shooting prowess earlier on.

'It is empty, but nearby I found something else.'

He picked up a small brass cartridge case from the floor and held it up. 'It is of the type used for this rifle. It appears that somebody fired a shot from in here, through this window' – he gestured to the sash window with the broken pane – into the drawing room opposite.'

Mrs Burward was breathing heavily. 'Oh lord,' she gasped. 'So whoever shot the master…'

'Was in this room,' said Zorard. 'Mrs Burward, please keep out of sight,' he added sharply, seeing that the housekeeper had wandered in front of the window.

'I'm sorry sir,' said Mrs Burward, stepping back towards the door. 'But what on earth are we going to do?'

'The situation is grave,' said Zorard. 'There are thieves and murderers outside willing to shoot anyone who attempts to leave. And the discovery of this rifle suggests something else.' He held up the weapon and looked in the direction of Elsie.

'Meaning what, exactly?' asked Elsie.

'Meaning,' said Zorard slowly, 'that we know of one person in this house who knows how to shoot such a rifle with great skill, and who was not in the room when His Majesty was shot.'

'That's slander!' hissed Elsie, stepping forward to confront Zorard. 'My future husband's just been shot dead by some…some foreign lunatics, and you think it was me that did it. Well there's one small problem with that theory.

What on earth would I have to gain from it?'

Shaw could see what direction this would take, and stepped forward to speak in a conciliatory tone. 'May I suggest we leave such matters to the police as and when we are able to summon them? Mr Zorard, would you please place the rifle in the gun cupboard – carefully, if you please – there may be fingerprints on it in addition to yours and Miss Garnham's.'

'I hope you're not suggesting anything as well, vicar,' said Elsie.

'Certainly not,' said Shaw. 'In addition to Mr Zorard and Soames, you are the only other person we can account for having touched that rifle. There is a chance, albeit a slim one, that other prints may be on it and they may prove valuable evidence.'

'You talk like a policeman,' said Ana.

'Let us just say I have had some experience of criminal matters,' said Shaw. He watched as Zorard gingerly placed the rifle in the gun cupboard and put the cartridge case beside it.

'Does anybody have a key to this cupboard?' asked Shaw.

'I'm sorry we don't, sir,' said Mrs Burward. 'I believe it was lost a while ago along with the key of the room. Major Chilcot got a bit absent minded in his old age.'

'Very well,' said Shaw. He looked at his watch. 'Mr Zorard, the time is drawing near where we must make a decision about our actions. We still have not searched the upper rooms.'

'You are right of course, Mr Shaw,' said Zorard. 'Come, we will check and lock the bedrooms.'

After they had searched the bedrooms, and even the attic rooms of The Larches, the group made its way back downstairs and huddled together in the corridor.

'Is there any room,' said Shaw to Zorard, 'which does not have a window?'

'There is only the billiard room, I think. Why do you ask?'

'I suggest we leave the womenfolk there,' said Shaw, 'as the safest place. They can barricade themselves in, while we prepare our course of action.'

'Oh thank you sir,' said Mrs Burward. 'That's the best thing I've heard. I don't feel safe all exposed like this. The billiard room's here.' She led the group to a door which she proceeded to unlock.

'Ladies, please stay inside this room and lock the door,' said Shaw, ushering the trio inside.

'Here, I don't like this,' said Elsie. 'Why should we consent to being locked up in here while you two gad about outside?'

'Miss Garnham, please do as you are told,' said Zorard firmly. 'Believe me, you do not wish to be involved with these people outside, if they are who I think they are.'

'That's as maybe,' said Elsie, 'but I'm not too happy about being stuck in there with her either.' She gestured to Ana. 'We've no idea what she's got to do with all this.'

'What do you mean?' asked Ana angrily.

'Don't you use that tone with me, young lady,' said Elsie. 'You just remember your place. I know nothing about you other than you're a Fenekslavian and from what I've seen of you lot I don't trust any of you.'

'Ladies, please,' said Shaw. 'I appreciate we are all on edge. It is natural to have suspicions. But we must not let these get out of hand. If you remain calm in the billiard room for the next half an hour or so that is all that is required.'

'And we can watch one another,' said Mrs Burward, who seemed to have recovered from her shock in the gun room, and found her old resolve again. She gestured for Elsie to sit down in a leather armchair. 'Come along madam. We can all watch one another and that way if anybody here is up to anything – I mention no names – we'll soon find out.'

*

'Come, Mr Shaw,' said Zorard. 'We will fetch the crown jewels. The hour is approaching.'

Zorard led the way to one of the rooms along the service corridor. 'This was His Majesty's private office,' he said. 'I have the key.' He took a key from his pocket and opened the door. He turned on a green-shaded light on a large desk and placed the poker he was holding on it. He then walked over to a large mahogany cupboard in the corner which he also unlocked, and took out a canvas holdall.

'These were smuggled out of Fenekslavia,' said Zorard, opening the bag and angling it towards Shaw.

Shaw caught a glimpse of a bejewelled crown and some sort of sceptre and chain. A large diamond suddenly caught a glint of moonlight from the window set high up in the wall; the precious stone glistened with almost other-wordly light.

'Pride of man and earthly glory,' whispered Shaw.

'What did you say?' asked Zorard, as he closed the bag.

'Nothing,' said Shaw. 'Merely the lines of a hymn.' He now realised why the tune had been going around in his head.

Pride of man and earthly glory
Sword and crown betray his trust
What with care and toil he buildeth
Tower and temple, turn to dust.

Were gold and jewels ever worth risking human happiness for?, thought Shaw. Never; they were in the end worthless dust; that was what the hymn told him.

'I must say, I am surprised at your change of heart,' said Shaw. 'You said earlier you would fight to the death to protect the crown jewels. I am pleased that you have seen sense; however valuable, they are not worth a human life.'

Zorard laughed briefly. 'You are a good priest, Mr Shaw. I, however, am not so good. Yes, I would fight to the death for the crown jewels. But these are not the real crown jewels of Fenekslavia. These are paste, replicas used for state occasions, brought along with the real ones when we escaped.'

'But then where are the real jewels?' asked Shaw, in amazement.

'In a safe deposit box in London, in the Ritz Hotel,' answered Zorard. 'I left them there after we arrived in this country. Do you really think I would leave such priceless items unguarded in a wardrobe?'

'I see,' said Shaw. 'But, will not the Bolsheviks notice the deception when they are handed over?'

Zorard laughed again, bitterly this time. 'These people are peasants, Mr Shaw. They will not tell the difference, at least not until experts in Fenekslavia examine them. How is it said in the Bible? The jewels shown to pigs.'

'Pearls before swine,' corrected Shaw. 'Very well. But please let us be careful. It would be even worse to be killed for imitation jewels than for real ones.'

'Quiet,' whispered Zorard. 'Did you hear that?'

Shaw felt the hairs on the back of his neck rise. He listened, and heard a shuffling sound outside the door.

'Somebody is outside,' said Zorard.

He picked up the poker and opened the door slowly. Once he had checked the corridor was clear, he crept out and motioned Shaw to follow.

The two men stood in the corridor, lit only by the silvery moonbeams falling through the window. A scraping sound came from outside. Zorard pressed himself against the wall by the window and raised his poker; Shaw did the same, raising the coal shovel in his hand which felt like an increasingly inadequate form of defence.

Shaw looked sideways into the courtyard and noticed, again, the pristine whiteness of the snow on the ground; although this time he noticed an unusual shadow, a sort of indentation in the snow, crossing between the gun room and the drawing room. He also saw footprints by the wall, which were rapidly disappearing under fresh snowfall.

The scraping sound became louder, and Shaw saw in the shadows of the brickwork, a figure edging his way toward the window. The figure stopped only inches away from Shaw's face and a black-clad arm slowly reached out in front of the window; fingers scrabbled under the window frame in an attempt to open it.

In one fluid movement Zorard hurled up the sash window and jerked the arm over the sill; the figure overbalanced and fell into the corridor with a howl of pain.

The two men looked down at the intruder sprawled on the stone floor of the corridor.

'You!' hissed Zorard.

Chapter Five

Keir Walters cursed as the little van's engine gave out a complaining whine and its wheels spun on the layer of snow and ice which coated the road to Lower Addenham. He remembered not to force the accelerator but instead gently eased it down until the wheels gripped and the van slithered back into motion.

The snow was falling more heavily now so he kept his speed down to ten miles an hour, which was all he dared risk. He would be late to collect Ana but at least she would able to wait in the warmth of the house before he arrived, rather than at the bus stop.

Sofia would be safe enough with his father until he got back; old Walters was absorbed in writing a long letter to Mr Gandhi asking him to ban meat-eating once the British Raj had been removed from power.

Keir had been pleased when Ana had mentioned the lucrative evening job she had got herself at The Larches, but at the same time was puzzled and wary. He knew she could not stand the former Fenekslavian king, so why work for him? He was worried she had some plan which could end badly. Fenekslavians were an odd lot, he recalled, from what he had seen of them during his time there. Blood feuds and ancient enmities, sometimes going back generations, were common. Ana had refused to be drawn on what she was going to do, but he guessed that it would involve more than just making meals for some deposed puppet monarch.

Keir had definitely had not liked the look of the man that had been in the café the other day – Zorro or something, he said his name was. He had seen his sort before when he was in Fenekslavia – swanning around Kecsprem or the seaside resort of Sevemapol, in motor cars or at café tables on the Parada Dremsca, smoking big cigars and clicking their fingers at the waiters.

The man had spoken to Ana in Fenekslavian and looked around the place as if he were lord of the manor, flicking through Crispin's pamphlets and even poking his nose into the back yard at one point.

Keir had been about to send him packing, but then Ana had introduced him as her new employer, so he had kept his feelings in check. But really, he thought, the revolution could not come too soon for people like that.

At least the British capitalist class had some romantic liberal ideas about treating the workers well and that sort of thing. It was all rot of course; a false front designed to salve their consciences and save their necks when the time came. But these eastern Europeans acted as if they had *droit de seigneur* and Ana, as an attractive young woman, could be easy prey.

He shivered and leaned forward to wipe the mist off the window of the unheated cab. Just then he heard the blare of a klaxon from behind and he had just enough time to pull the wheel to the left as a little Morris two-seater, flashing its headlamps on and off, shot past him.

'Blasted idiot!' shouted Keir, only narrowly managing to avoid landing the van in a ditch. Just his luck to come across a road-hog on a night like this, he thought.

A few minutes later he had recovered his composure, with the help of a Woodbine, and was pleased to see the front gate of The Larches looming up ahead, the stone lions on the gateposts faintly illuminated by the beam of the van's headlamps.

Keir was minded to open the main gates and drive straight up to the front of the house, but he did not want to risk antagonising Ana's new employer, especially one who paid as well as he did. He drove on a little way further and turned into the lane which led to the tradesman's entrance set in the high hedge which surrounded the grounds of The Larches.

He parked the little van as far onto the snow-encrusted verge as he dared and turned off the engine. Strictly speaking he was supposed to keep the headlamps lit while parked on the road at night, but he did not want to run down the battery and anyway, he reflected, the chance of any nosey policemen passing this way at night just to give him a ten-bob fine seemed slim.

As he stepped out of the cab he actually felt warmer as his body began to generate a little heat from moving. He crossed to the little tradesman's gate and pressed the electrical bell push which, he assumed, rang somewhere in the bowels of the house beyond.

Nobody came and after a few minutes, he rang again; from what he could see of the house beyond, there were no lights on. He looked at his watch; Ana was supposed to have finished work at least half an hour ago if not more, once tea had been served. After a final long push on the bell, he muttered to himself.

'Blow this for a game of soldiers. I'm going in.'

He tried the handle of the gate, expecting it to be locked, but it swung open. He stepped through and began to walk up the little path to the house. His shoes made a crunching, creaking sound which seemed much louder than it ought to have done.

For a moment, Keir glimpsed movement out of the corner of his eye, but before he had time to turn towards it, his vision was obliterated by a gloved hand pressed into his face; he felt something trip his legs from under him and he saw the white ground rushing towards him until he collided with it in an explosion of stars.

*

'Give me one good reason why I should not shoot you like a dog,' said Zorard, shaking the shoulders of Soames as he lay on the floor of the corridor. 'Creeping around the house like a vampire. Was it you who shot His Majesty? Are you working with the Bolsheviks? Speak!'

Zorard gripped his poker firmly and raised it to strike Soames. His arm was gently pushed back by Shaw's hand.

'Mr Zorard, please. Stop. The man is terrified.'

'So he should be,' said Zorard, but he lowered his arm.

'Let us remain calm, and let him speak,' said Shaw.

'I...I didn't know what to do, sir,' said Soames, who looked wild-eyed with fear at Zorard and then Shaw.

'Where have you been?' asked Shaw. 'Quickly man,' he added, sensing Soames' reluctance to speak. 'We need to establish your innocence before we can release you.'

'I went down to fetch more tea,' said Soames, 'but when I was just about to come out of the kitchen I heard a window break and then shooting. Then I heard somebody running along the corridor towards me, so I locked the door.'

'And you did not even dare to look?' hissed Zorard. 'You coward, that was only Mrs Burward running to the telephone.'

'I'm sorry sir,' whined Soames, 'only how could I have known that?'

'Why didn't you call out?' asked Shaw.

'I...truth be told I was too scared to, sir,' said the butler, with a shamefaced expression. Zorard looked at him in disgust.

'Never mind, Soames, go on,' said Shaw.

'Yes sir, well I came out of the kitchen once the coast was clear and had a look outside.'

'Why did you not come to us in the drawing room?' demanded Zorard.

'I had no idea what was going on and didn't dare risk it, sir. I thought if a window had been broken there might be intruders outside, so I checked there first.'

'Too scared to come to the drawing room, but brave enough to go outside in the dark?' said Zorard. 'I don't believe you.' He raised his hand, empty of the poker this time, towards Soames' face.

'Now, Mr Zorard, please,' insisted Shaw firmly. 'People do not always act rationally under interrogation. Will you kindly allow me to continue questioning Mr Soames without the threat of violence?'

'Very well,' grumbled Zorard, releasing his grip from Soames' lapels and standing up. 'But hurry. We do not have much time before the demands of the assassins must be met.'

'Thank you sir,' said Soames to Shaw with relief in his voice. He stood up and dusted himself down, regaining some of his butler-like composure.

'I wasn't acting rationally, I suppose,' he said. 'I had a look outside in the courtyard, and saw the window to the drawing room was broken, and when I peeped round the side I saw…well, I saw what looked like the king lying on the floor, with a cloth over his face. Is he…?'

'Dead, yes,' said Shaw bluntly. 'Somebody shot him through the window. We believe it to have been Bolshevik assassins.'

Soames swallowed hard. 'I thought it might be something like that,' he said. 'That's why I didn't come back in the front door. I saw the king lying there, nobody about, and so I said to myself there must be a madman on the loose. I dashed back into the hallway to telephone for the police, but the phone was dead. Then I thought, nothing for it, I'll have to make a dash to the garage.'

'Tell me, Soames,' said Zorard, 'were you able to telephone the police from there?'

Soames looked crestfallen. 'No sir. I'm sorry sir, I never actually got there. I lost my nerve.'

'It is no matter,' said Zorard. 'We have no idea how many of the enemy are outside, and they have probably cut the telephone lines to the garage anyway. Now we will have no choice but to…how is it the English say? "Bite the bullet"'.

Shaw looked at his watch and nodded. 'Indeed,' he said. 'We have only a few minutes left.'

Soames looked from Shaw to Zorard and then back again. 'I take it there is a plan of action, gentlemen. Might I be of any assistance in carrying it out?'

'You appear to be a perfect coward, but I still don't trust you,' said Zorard. 'I have a plan but at present Mr Shaw is the only person whom I trust to help carry it out. You can stay in the billiard room with the women. We will escort you there ourselves.'

*

Mrs Shaw was worried. Although her husband had only specified that he would be back 'around five pm', it was now some time after that. The snow had been falling for a while and it was pitch black outside; she imagined him sprawled in a ditch, with his broken bicycle beside him, the front wheel spinning slowly.

Of course it was silly, she thought, but she decided that to be on the safe side she would telephone to The Larches to enquire if he had left yet. If truth be told she was also hoping that she might speak to the king in person, but then told herself he would hardly be answering the telephone himself.

That was when she began to be more worried. Not only did the king not answer the telephone – nobody did. She asked the woman at the little local exchange to try to connect her twice, and each time she was told the number was unobtainable.

'Is everything alright, madam?' asked Hettie, who noted the look of concern on Mrs Shaw's face as she replaced the telephone receiver on the little hall table.

'Would you be awfully good and run down to Thorpe's at the station?' said Mrs Shaw. 'He's not answering the telephone either.'

'The little taxi office, madam?'

'Yes,' said Mrs Shaw. 'Ask him if he can bring his car round. I'd go myself but I want to stay here in case Mr Shaw telephones.'

'Very good, madam,' said Hettie. 'I'll only be five minutes.'

Hettie was true to her word and five minutes later returned. She emerged from the kitchen, which she had entered via the back door.

'I'm sorry madam,' she said. 'But there's a sign on the door of the office saying closed early due to inclement weather.'

'Oh dear,' said Mrs Shaw, twisting her pearl necklace around her finger, a little habit she had when nervous. Then inspiration hit her.

'Thank you Hettie, that will be all,' she said. 'You can get on with making the dinner now.'

'Very good madam,' said Hettie with a bob, and disappeared into the kitchen.

Mrs Shaw consulted a little book on the hall table and then picked up the telephone. 'Addenham 663,' she said to the operator, and then waited to be connected.

'Is that you, Peggy?' she asked a moment later.

Her friend Peggy Marchant answered in her usual brusque, no-nonsense voice. 'Yes, who's that speaking, please?'

'It's Marion.'

'Hello old girl,' said Mrs Marchant. 'How's things with you?'

Mrs Shaw heard the click of a cigarette lighter and a sharp inhalation of breath. Mrs Marchant, she remembered, was a keen smoker and used one of those tortoiseshell cigarette holders, clamped between her teeth like a man smoking a pipe.

'Oh, very well thank you Peggy.'

'And the Padre?'

'Well…that's why I've called. This will sound awfully silly.'

Mrs Marchant chuckled. 'I very much doubt it. Whole bally world's gone potty in the last few years, as far as I can see. I doubt anything would surprise me. Come on old girl, what's on your mind?'

'Lucian was visiting The Larches and he hasn't come back yet.'

'The Larches? Isn't that the place where that chap, whatshisname, ex-king or sultan of somewhere is supposed to be living?'

'That's it. Well Lucian went there for a sort of, sort of parish visit, and he should have been back by now.'

'Probably just held up by this snow. On his bicycle, was he?'

'Yes.'

'Well then. I expect he's just pushing the thing carefully instead of riding. Or got a puncture perhaps.'

'I thought of that, but when I telephoned to The Larches to ask if he'd gone, there was no reply, and the girl at the exchange said the number was out of order.'

'Hmm, alright then,' said Mrs Marchant, 'Tell you what. I'll get the old bus out and we'll tootle along there and probably see him on the lane. There's plenty of room in the car for his bicycle.'

'Oh, thank you so much Peggy,' said Mrs Shaw with a sigh of relief. She was glad she had not had to ask directly for a lift. 'I tried getting a taxi but they've closed early.'

'Doesn't surprise me in the least,' said Mrs Marchant with a sigh. 'One flake of snow nowadays and people decide to stay indoors. Now when I was driving ambulances in the war, we…'

'I'll see you in a few minutes then,' Mrs Shaw interrupted, not wishing to hear yet another of her friend's reminiscences of her time in the First Aid Nursing Yeomanry.

A few minutes later Mrs Shaw, with Fraser held in her arms for warmth, was installed in Mrs Marchant's Singer

Senior motor car. The solidly built and somewhat jowly Mrs Marchant appeared even more solid than usual, dressed as she was in an enormous fur coat and rather masculine brown hat with a large feather in the brim.

'Good job I decided not to bring Brutus,' said Mrs Marchant, referring to her enormous mastiff. 'He'd eat your little tyke alive.'

Fraser barked and Mrs Marchant patted him on the head. 'There there Fraser,' she said in a consoling voice. 'I know you punch well above your weight.'

'Do keep your hands on the wheel, Peggy,' said Mrs Shaw nervously. 'It's so awfully icy.'

'Don't worry old girl,' said Mrs Marchant. 'I've driven through worse than this.' She clamped her teeth down harder on her cigarette holder and peered forward as another flurry of snow blew across the windscreen. The lane leading to The Larches was dark, and visibility was down to just a few yards.

Mrs Marchant pointed with one gloved finger out of the windscreen.

'Hello,' she said. 'Is this him?'

Mrs Shaw saw a man in a long dark overcoat and homburg hat, standing by the tall hedge which surrounded the outer edges of The Larches' estate.

'I don't think so,' she said, 'and why is he just standing there?'

'Soon find out,' said Mrs Marchant. She stopped the car by the man, who looked around in surprise.

Mrs Marchant opened her window a little way. 'Sorry to trouble you,' she said to the man, 'but you haven't seen an errant parson coming along this way on a bicycle, have you?'

The man's face was largely in shadow, lit from the side by the reflected glow of the car's headlamps in the snow. It was an odd looking face, thought Mrs Shaw, a sallow colour with high cheekbones. It was not a friendly face, and nor, she thought, was it an English one.

The man glowered at them and shook his head, then looked behind himself quickly at the hedge. He made a shoo-ing away movement with his hand towards the lane.

'I'm not quite sure what that gesture is intended to mean,' said Mrs Marchant, in the sort of icy patrician tone that she used to wither disrespectful shopmen. 'I will assume you mean you saw somebody going in that direction,' she continued. 'Perhaps you will be good enough to confirm it vocally.'

Just then there was a sound of rustling leaves and another man, dressed similarly in black, emerged from the hedgerow.

'What on earth are you doing?' exclaimed Mrs Marchant.

'Oh Peggy,' said Mrs Shaw. 'I don't like this. Let's drive on, quickly.' She clutched Fraser tightly as he bared his teeth and growled at the men outside the car.

'I shall report this,' said Mrs Marchant, closing the window. 'Blasted poachers,' she said to Mrs Shaw. 'Probably looking for pheasants. I'll tell the constable once we get back. He...'

Just then the back doors of the car were pulled open and the two men jumped in, slamming the doors behind them.

'What the...get out this instant!' roared Mrs Marchant, and for a brief moment Mrs Shaw saw their shadowed faces flinch back. Then one of the men raised his gloved hand and in it, a dark object gleamed.

'He's got a gun!' said Mrs Shaw. Fraser bared his teeth and yelped twice at the men, but she held him close to her chest.

Mrs Marchant's eyes flicked to the rear view mirror. The tone of her voice changed to that which she had used to calm the hysterical people she had sometimes encountered while she was an ambulance driver during the Zeppelin raids.

'All right, all right,' she said. 'No need to get excited. My bag's on the back seat next to you. There's five pounds in it. We won't say anything to the police.'

'Drive,' said one of the men in a guttural voice.

'Very well,' said Mrs Marchant.

Mrs Shaw's hands trembled and she pressed Fraser closer to herself; he continued to emit a low growl at the men. He then barked loudly, letting out a series of threatening yelps. One of the men leaned forward and tried to cuff him, then recoiled with a yell as Fraser's sharp little teeth, a product of centuries of breeding for the killing of rodents, bit into his hand.

The man shouted something incomprehensible and jumped back, sprawling on top of the man with the gun. Mrs Marchant opened her door and shouted.

'Run!'

Without pausing for thought Mrs Shaw scrabbled for the door handle and jumped out, running around to the opposite side to be with Mrs Marchant. She saw her friend turn to the back door of the car and open it. The two men had still not managed to disentangle themselves; the one with the gun was trying to point it at Mrs Marchant through the door. She kicked at his arm with one heavily brogued foot but he did not drop the pistol. Seeing this, she reached forward and slammed the door closed as hard as she could, crushing the man's fingers.

He screamed in agony and dropped the pistol onto the snow. Fraser, who was still in the car, was pulling at the coat collar of one of the men with terrific force. Realising his pistol was out of reach, the man appeared to panic and pushed his companion out of the opposite door. They ran along the lane with Fraser running and barking behind them. Within seconds they had driven off in a small saloon car half-hidden in the hedgerow.

'Brutes!' shouted Mrs Marchant, picking up the pistol. With no experience of firearms, she did not dare try to shoot at them and besides, they were now out of sight, leaving only a cloud of exhaust fumes and a thin trail of vivid blood in the snow behind them.

'Are you alright, Marion?' she said, getting her breath back and turning to her companion.

'I think so,' said Mrs Shaw. 'Do you mind awfully if I sit down?'

She felt her knees give way, and sat down in the passenger seat of the car, with the door open. Fraser, who had given up trying to chase the car, arrived and jumped into Mrs Shaw's arms. He was holding some dark object in his mouth but dropped it at her feet, and then began licking her face.

'Good boy Fraser, good boy,' she said, forcing herself to remain calm. 'I say, I'm shaking like a leaf.'

'Natural reaction,' said Mrs Marchant, retaining some of her usual composure. 'Stiff drink's what you need. Brandy in the glove compartment. Johnny keeps it there to keep the cold out while driving. Could do with one myself.'

Praising Mr John Marchant's foresight, Mrs Shaw took a little silver flask out of the glove compartment and gave it to Mrs Marchant. She took a large swig and passed it to Mrs Shaw, who hesitated slightly.

'Go on,' said Mrs Marchant. 'Best thing for shock.'

Mrs Shaw sipped some of the strong liquid and felt a warming glow immediately. She passed the flask back to

Mrs Marchant who took another draft then snapped the lid shut.

'Right,' said Mrs Marchant. 'Plan of action. We'll drive to The Larches and telephone for the police to tell them about those blasted thugs. Then we'll telephone to your house – and if the Padre isn't back we'll report him missing.'

The two women climbed back into the car. Mrs Marchant placed the pistol gingerly on the back seat.

'You don't think,' said Mrs Shaw, as they drove along the lane, 'you don't think there's any connection between Lucian not coming home and those two men? They didn't look like poachers.'

'Now now, Marion, let's not jump to conclusions,' said Mrs Marchant. 'The Padre's most likely got held up at The Larches or he took some other way home. First thing to do is to inform the police about those men. And you're right, I don't think they were poachers. I think we may have disturbed a burglary.'

'What a dreadful thought,' said Mrs Shaw, taking a deep breath. 'And I just sat here cowering.'

'Nonsense, you kept calm, that's the main thing. I probably should have done the same but I rather lost my temper after having a gun pointed at me. That filthy blighter won't be playing the violin for a while anyway.'

'I did at least manage to get the number,' said Mrs Shaw.

'Number?'

'Yes, of that car those men got away in.'

'Good girl. What was it?'

'BJ 193. Or was it 198? Oh dear, I can't remember.'

'Never mind, that should be enough for the police to go on.'

'In all the confusion I forgot about this,' said Mrs Shaw, bending down to pick up the dark object that Fraser had dropped in the footwell. It was a torn glove. Mrs Shaw shuddered with distaste as she looked down to see her fingers smeared with blood.

'It must have come off that man,' she said.

'Put it with the pistol,' said Mrs Marchant. 'Could be a valuable clue. We can mention that to the police when we telephone. Nearly there now.'

The car stopped in front of the gates of The Larches.

'Hmm, looks like a bell or something on the gate. I'll ring it,' said Mrs Marchant. She got out of the car and pressed the electric bell-push by the gates and waited.

In the car, Mrs Shaw turned to place the scrap of glove with the pistol. By the dim light of the vehicle's instrument panel, she could just about see a small embroidered maker's label on the edge of the glove. She peered closely but could not make it out. Then she looked again and realised it was written in some foreign language. Polish perhaps, or something Scandinavian. She placed the scrap next to the pistol and bit her lower lip with worry.

Mrs Marchant opened the gates and got back into the car.

'Nobody answering the bell,' she said. 'Can't see any lights on in the house either. Don't like the look of this.'

Mrs Shaw felt panic rising in her chest and fought to keep it down, stroking Fraser to calm herself. The car edged slowly along the snow-covered drive.

A dazzling light appeared momentarily in front of them and Mrs Shaw gasped as a dark figure stepped out in front of the car with his hand raised. Mrs Marchant slammed on the brakes.

'What now?' she said.

Before Mrs Shaw had a chance to reply, both doors of the car were wrenched open, and the two women turned to see large revolvers pointed at their heads, held in the gloved hands of two men with hats pulled down over their eyes.

Chapter Six

'Let me in please, it is I, Zorard.' The voice came from behind the door of the billiard room in which Elsie, Ana and Mrs Burward had secured themselves. They had locked the door and pushed a large table in front of it for extra protection.

After they had removed the obstacle and Mrs Burward had unlocked the door, Zorard, Shaw and Soames appeared.

'Oh Mr Soames,' said Mrs Burward. 'I'm glad to see you're alright. What happened to you?'

'He can explain to you,' said Zorard briskly. 'For now, he will wait with you. Please barricade yourselves in again and if you do not hear anything from us within an hour, you must assume the worst.'

'What's going to happen?' asked Elsie suspiciously.

'Mr Shaw and I will leave the crown jewels on the front step as instructed by the assassins. Once they have been taken we must remain here until dawn before going for help.'

'If you think I'm going to stay here,' said Elsie, 'while my fiance's body is lying next door and his killers are lurking outside, you...'

'Miss Garnham, please,' said Zorard, raising his hand. 'I know it is difficult but I cannot risk the safety of you or any others. We must do what these people say.'

'I also do not wish to stay. I have a young daughter, my husband will be getting worried,' said Ana.

'Didn't you say he was coming to collect you in his van?' asked Mrs Burward.

Ana's face fell. 'I forgot. Yes. He should be here by now. Why is he not here? What if...?'

'There, there dear, don't worry,' said Mrs Burward. 'I'm sure he's alright. Probably just held up by the snow. '

'This could be to our advantage,' said Shaw. 'If Mr Walters sees suspicious activity outside on his arrival, he may become concerned and telephone the police.'

'It is a slim hope,' said Zorard, 'and one that we cannot rely on. Come, Mr Shaw, it is almost time.'

'Very well,' replied Shaw, turning to follow Zorard who was striding out into the corridor. 'Mr Soames, you are in charge. Please see that no harm comes to the womenfolk.' With that he closed the door.

Mrs Burward locked the door and she and Soames pushed the table back to block the entrance.

Ana, standing behind the sofa, watched and reflected that she was not at all confident in Soames' ability to defend them from Fenekslavian assassins.

'And where were you, Mr Soames, in our hour of need?' asked Mrs Burward, folding her arms and looking at him suspiciously as she stood guard by the door.

'I was trying to telephone for help at the garage,' said Soames, defensively. He hovered awkwardly between the door and the sofa on which Elsie was sitting. 'But the place was crawling with Bolshies and I didn't dare risk it.'

'Really?' said Elsie. 'How many did you see?'

'Oh, dozens,' said Soames, after some hesitation.

Mrs Burward scoffed. 'I don't believe you Mr Soames. Why, this is England. We don't have Russians marching around the countryside killing people.'

'They are not Russians. They are Fenekslavians,' said Ana.

'Well,' said Mrs Burward, 'I still don't believe it. There might be one or two but not legions of them.'

'I think there might even just be one of them,' said Elsie, looking at Ana.

Ana caught her glance and her eyes flashed fire. 'Do you mean something about me?' she said.

'What I find odd,' continued Elsie to Ana, 'is how you appeared out of nowhere to work here, and then my poor Basil got shot dead while you were out of the room.'

'You accuse me, you…' hissed Ana.

'Tsk, girl, remember who you are talking to,' chided Mrs Burward.

'It's alright, Mrs Burward,' said Elsie. 'I'd like to hear what she's got to say. Remind me what your name is again, dear.'

'Ana Walters.'

'Ana dear,' replied Elsie, 'speak your mind. I'm listening.'

'You accuse me,' said Ana, 'yet it also could have been you who killed…that man. Even Zorard said so. There was a rifle and a, how do you call it, an empty bullet case in that room opposite. We all saw it. You were not in the room when the shot was fired either.'

Elsie laughed throatily. 'I think that's a bit of a tall tale. I found a little piece of evidence to show it was pretty unlikely for me to have shot Basil.'

Ana noticed that Soames, who was almost out of earshot and whose expression until now had been one of bland professionalism, suddenly looked interested.

'Did I hear you mention something to me, madam ?'

'No you did not,' replied Elsie. 'For now I suggest we stop the polite conversation and concentrate on getting out of here.'

Soames looked worried. 'The gentlemen said we were to stay in this room.'

Elsie laughed again. 'I'm not sitting here while some Red with snow on his boots steals what's rightfully mine.'

'The crown jewels of Fenekslavia are not yours,' said Ana firmly.

'I think we'll let the law decide that.' replied Elsie with icy politeness. 'Matter of fact, I think I may even have a case to become Queen of Fenekslavia anyway. What do they call the widow of a king?'

'Queen Dowager,' said Mrs Burward. 'But with respect madam, you weren't yet married.'

'We'll see about that,' replied Elsie. 'Monty – that's my agent, Monty Samuels – knows all sorts of legal people in London. I think it could be worth a try.'

Ana, who did not feel confident enough to argue the legal rights of a dead king's fiancée, kept quiet.

'Right then,' said Elsie, standing up. 'That's enough talking. I'm getting out of here.'

'But Mr Zorard said…' protested Soames.

'That Zorard and that parson are a couple of drips for handing over the loot, if you ask me,' said Elsie. 'I'm going to stop whoever tries to take those jewels.'

'But how can you stop them?' said Soames. 'They'll be armed.'

'So will I,' said Elsie. 'I'm going to the gun room and I'll pick up a shotgun.'

'But madam,' said Mrs Burward, 'there aren't any bullets. Whoever shot the king took them all from the gun room. Mr Zorard said so.'

'I know that,' said Elsie. 'But whoever took the cartridges from the gun room didn't know about these.' She took two shotgun cartridges from the pocket of her tweed hunting jacket and displayed them to the group.

'I put them in my pocket during the shoot and forgot about them. I only noticed them just now. I doubt there's more than two men out there and these will be enough for me to stop them. I'll need help to grab the bag though, so who's with me?'

'I will help,' said Ana firmly. 'Then maybe you will realise I am not part of this crime of killing the king.'

'That's for the police to decide,' said Elsie, 'but for now I'll be glad of your assistance.'

'I'm with you as well, madam,' said Mrs Burward, folding her arms resolutely. 'My husband died to keep the Huns out of England and I'm blowed if I'll sit by while another lot of brutes thinks they can march in.'

The three women moved towards the door. Soames stood in front of it.

'My orders were to keep you in here,' he said firmly.

'Out of the way Soames,' said Elsie. 'You can cower in here if you like but we're getting out. Now, help me move this table.'

Soames stepped forward with a determined look on his face. He reached inside his morning coat and pulled out a revolver which he pointed at Elsie's midriff.

'I'm sorry about this,' he said, 'but you are all to remain here. It's for your own safety.'

For the first time Elsie appeared shocked. 'Soames…what are you doing?' she asked. 'Where did you get that gun?'

'My name isn't Soames,' said the butler, in a voice stripped of its former obsequiousness. 'We can drop all that now.'

'Who are you then?' said Mrs Burward angrily. 'I knew there was something rum about you. You're about the worst butler I ever worked with.'

'Quiet,' snapped the man. 'Sit down, all of you, where I can see you.' He waved the pistol in the direction of the sofa.

'You're...you're one of them,' said Elsie slowly.

'You know nothing about me or what you're getting yourself into,' said the man impatiently. 'Now *sit down*, all of you.'

Elsie and Mrs Burward backed towards the sofa; the man momentarily looked at them, turning his head away from Ana. In that instant, she seized a heavy trophy from the sideboard, one belonging to the late Major Chilcot, Indian Army Billiards Champion of 1893.

She smashed it down hard on the man's head. The revolver clattered heavily on the parquet floor as he dropped it, and a moment later he fell down beside it in a crumpled heap, groaned, and then became silent.

'Oh Lord,' exclaimed Mrs Burward. 'I think you've killed him!'

*

Zorard and Shaw retrieved the bag of jewels from the king's office and made their way to the front door. Zorard stopped and spoke in a low tone.

'You have been most helpful, Mr Shaw, but please, you must now go back and join the others.'

'I am concerned that you may require assistance,' said Shaw. 'What if the assassins decide to go back on their promise, and attack you?'

'Then there is very little you will be able to do to help,' said Zorard, shaking his head with regret. 'Ach, if only I were armed. Then these animals would not get away with this.'

'Let us at least be thankful that the real crown jewels are safe,' said Shaw. 'And I have an idea of how I may be able to assist in the capture of the criminals.'

'Mr Shaw, please,' said Zorard, putting his hand on the latch of the front door. The hallway was dark, and he peered through one of the side windows out into the driveway. 'It is not worth putting yourself at risk for imitation jewels.'

'I am not concerned about the jewels,' said Shaw. 'I am concerned that the king's killers are still at large.'

'Very well,' replied Zorard. He looked through the side window again. 'The way seems clear but they will probably have concealed themselves in the bushes. Please go back to the billiard room, before I open the door.'

'Please hear me out, Mr Zorard,' said Shaw. 'I intend to leave by the back door and follow whoever takes the jewels, at a safe distance.'

'I cannot allow it,' insisted Zorard. 'Remember, I was shot at while trying to leave by that door.'

'I will leave by a window,' said Shaw. 'They will not expect that, and besides, they will be concentrating on the other side of the house.'

Zorard sighed. 'But the womenfolk....'

'They are barricaded in the billiard room, and safe enough,' said Shaw. 'It is vital that one of us gets help. I can do this and at the same time, track the movements of the thieves. They will probably have a motor car nearby, and I may be able to see the number plate.'

Zorard sighed. 'Very well, I see that you are a man of courage and persistence. Go then. But keep out of sight.'

'Very well,' said Shaw. 'Good luck, and God be with you.'

Shaw walked to the end of the hallway into the corridor that led to the back door, remembering that he had seen a window there previously.

Zorard silently opened the front door and placed the bag of jewels on the step.

*

'He's still breathing,' said Elsie, looking down at the man lying on the floor of the billiard room whom they knew only as Soames.

'Oh thank the Lord,' said Mrs Burward. 'We've had enough killing for one day in this house.'

'You took a bit of a risk doing that,' said Elsie to Ana.

'He could have killed us,' replied Ana defiantly. 'I will not go in fear of these people.'

'Well you've got some pluck dear, I'll give you that,' said Elsie. 'Now let's get out of here quick, and get to the gun room.' She turned to the door and began to push the heavy table aside.

'Shouldn't we ought to tie him up, or something?' asked Mrs Burward, looking doubtfully at the man on the floor as she helped Elsie with the table.

'There isn't time,' said Elsie. 'And anyway, what would we use?'

The three women looked around the room and saw nothing with which they could tie him.

'We'll just have to lock him in,' said Elsie. 'There's no window in here so he can't get out. Now come on, we'll go to the gun room and then go round the outside of the house to stop anyone taking those jewels off the front step.'

'I will go alone,' said Ana. 'I will follow those who take the jewels and find where they go. If you try to stop them they may kill you.'

'Don't be silly, girl,' said Mrs Burward anxiously. 'You stay with us. Madam's an expert shot and we'll be in good hands.'

'I do not trust her,' said Ana.

Elsie laughed. 'Well if it comes to that I don't trust you either dear, but I'm the only one with the shotgun cartridges.'

'I also have this,' said Ana. She produced the revolver that Soames had dropped and which she had been holding behind her back.

'I'd forgotten all about that in the excitement,' said Elsie. Then she turned to face Ana. 'For God's sake don't point guns at people,' she said.

There was a pause, as Ana looked down at the pistol and then at Elsie.

'Give it to me dear,' said Elsie gently. 'It's cocked. We don't want it going off accidentally, do we?'

Ana reluctantly handed the weapon over to Elsie, who uncocked it then examined it. 'British Army issue service revolver. Bit of an odd choice for a Bolshevik spy. Could be stolen, I suppose.' She then checked the chamber, spun it and closed it. 'Six rounds. We won't need to bother with the gun room now. Unless you want to take a shotgun.'

'No, I do not know how to use one,' said Ana. 'But I am still going to go on my own,' said Ana. 'We will have more chance to get away.'

'Alright dear, maybe you've got a point,' said Elsie. She looked at her watch. 'Those jewels are supposed to be on the front step by now. Come on Mrs Burward, you come with me and we'll try to stop whoever it is getting their hands on them. Ana, you keep apart from us and if anything happens to us, you go for help.'

Ana nodded and the three women moved cautiously out into the corridor. Soames was beginning to moan and move slightly. They closed the door and, with a jingling of keys, Mrs Burward ensured that it was locked.

*

In the dark back corridor leading from the kitchens and servants' quarters, Shaw found the window he had remembered seeing earlier. Breathing a sigh of relief that it was not locked, he raised the sash as slowly as he could to avoid any squeaks or rattles. Once the window was open to its fullest extent, he paused. An icy breeze swept into the room, blowing a few errant snowflakes inside which rapidly melted on the relative warmth of the stone floor.

All was quiet outside. Shaw noticed the coats and hats on the pegs by the back door and realised that one of the hats was his own, put there by Soames on his arrival at lunch time, which now seemed a lifetime away.

There was also an umbrella stand of the type made out of an old artillery shell case, with a couple of umbrellas and a walking stick in it. The military article reminded him of an old trick he had seen in his army chaplaincy days. He took one of the umbrellas from the stand, and his hat down from the peg, and placed his hat on the tip of the umbrella.

He crouched under the window and cautiously raised the hat over the edge of the sill, to give the appearance of somebody looking out. All remained quiet, and no shots came. He lowered the hat and raised it again, but still nothing happened.

After a deep breath and a quick prayer, Shaw clambered quickly out of the window and dropped onto a gravel path. Crouching low, he immediately ran into the cover of some bushes close by and pressed his body and head into the frozen ground, expecting the whizz and ping of bullets around him at any moment. Nothing happened.

Shaw allowed his eyes to adjust to the dark and then scanned the surrounding undergrowth and the lawn beyond for signs of movement. There was an icily bright moon in the sky which went in and out of view as clouds drifted across it. Shaw noticed that the crisp snow upon the path and lawn at the back of the house was undisturbed, but there was still the possibility that a sniper was hiding in the hedgerow.

He decided he would stay close to the house, in the cover of the undergrowth, and edge his way around to the closest point to the rear service gate; he could just make it out in the distance, its black railings set against the white backdrop of the snow-covered lane beyond. Once through that he would be able to reach the telephone box, put through a call to Lower Addenham police station, and then secret himself in a vantage point at the junction, so that he would be able to see anyone trying to leave by the front or rear gate of the house.

He prayed that the telephone would work, and then wondered whether the assassins would have thought of such a plan and put a guard on the box, or perhaps disabled it in the same way they had cut the telephone lines to the house. He put such pessimistic thoughts out of his head and began to crawl along the side of the house, stopping every few seconds to listen intently for the sounds of any approaching assailant.

After crawling a few yards the undergrowth gave out and Shaw realised he was near the back door. He realised he would have to cross the short expanse of the back drive and lawn before he could reach the relative safety of the undergrowth on the other side of the doorway. He lay down under the cover of the bushes, squinting ahead to try to see any movement before he made a dash for it.

In a brief moment when the snow-covered rear path was illuminated by the moon, he saw footprints on the back step. Zorard's, presumably, from when he had attempted to get out of the house earlier, and had been driven back by gunfire. There were other patterns on the snow near the back step, suggesting someone had swept it. It was almost as if someone had been scooping up the white powder to make snowballs. What a queer notion, thought Shaw; then he concluded that Zorard must have fallen to the ground for cover once the shots rang out.

Shaw noticed something half buried in the snow glinting in the moonlight. He gingerly reached out from the undergrowth and snatched it. He turned it over in his hand and, as far as he could tell in the dim light, it was a little brass cartridge case. Thinking that it could be valuable evidence, he pocketed it.

He then took a deep breath and got to his feet, emerged from the undergrowth and sprinted across the open ground in front of the door. No shots came, and he dived into the rhododendron bush on the other side of the door. There was more space inside this undergrowth, and he was able to walk rather than crawl.

He froze. From the back door came the sounds of movement and low voices. Through the leaves of the bushes he could not see the back door, only the back step from the side. To his horror, he saw a hand emerge from the doorway, pointing a pistol; moments later two huddled figures emerged from the doorway and dashed into the bushes next to him. His wind was knocked out of him as he fell to the ground, and he gasped for breath as he felt the hard pistol barrel pressed into his ribs.

Shaw saw a flash of peroxide blonde hair and caught a whiff of scent. He looked into the face of his assailant. It was Elsie Garnham.

'For the Lord's sake,' hissed another voice, 'don't shoot him madam. It's the vicar.'

'Sorry vicar,' whispered Elsie, who withdrew the pistol from Shaw's ribs, allowing him to sit up and retain some form of composure. 'What are you doing creeping about in the bushes?'

'I might ask you the same question, Miss Garnham,' whispered Shaw, 'and where did you get that gun?'

'Listen, why should I trust you?' replied Elsie. 'You could be involved in all this.'

'Oh madam,' whispered Mrs Burward. 'He's been vicar here for years. He's not involved in anything.'

'All right,' said Elsie. 'I suppose I've got to trust you. I got the gun from the butler,' replied Elsie. 'He's in with whoever did for Basil. But we put him out of action and now we're going to do the same to anyone who tries to get away with those jewels. What about you?'

Shaw was about to tell Elsie and Mrs Burward about the jewels being only paste, but something made him keep this information to himself. 'My plan is to get to the telephone box in the lane,' he said, 'and after summoning help, find a vantage point to watch for any vehicle which attempts to leave the premises.'

'Good plan, vicar,' said Elsie. 'You can make a dash for the back gate. I'll cover you then Mrs Burward and I will make our way round to watch the front of the house to join Ana.'

'You mean Mrs Walters is alone?' asked Shaw.

'I didn't want her to go off like that but she wouldn't listen,' said Elsie.

'I can't say as I trust her much, sir,' added Mrs Burward. 'It wouldn't surprise me if she…'

'No matter,' interjected Shaw. 'We have no time to lose. Very well, Miss Garnham, please give covering fire if I require it. I shall run to the gate.'

'Righto vicar,' said Elsie. 'Good luck to you.'

'And to you,' said Shaw. He took a deep breath and then sprinted across the lawn. His body tensed with the expectation of the agonising impact of a bullet at any moment.

Before he had managed to reach the back gate, the white lawn was suddenly bathed in light from the house; there was the sound of a sash window being thrown up and then the shrill blast of a police whistle. A confused sound of shouting came from behind him.

Before he could get within twelve yards of the gate, two black-clad figures emerged from the hedgerow on either side. He was dazzled by electric torches; colours swam before his eyes and he blinked; the men were pointing pistols at him and shouting incomprehensibly.

To stop now is death, thought Shaw, and he focused all his efforts on reaching the gate. He reached out his arm to open it, but his legs gave way as somebody rugby-tackled him from behind. Sharp icicles dug into his cheek as his face was pressed into the frozen ground by the weight of a man on top of him. Shaw struggled desperately, but the man held his neck in a vice-like grip.

'Now you stay put like a good gentleman,' said a gruff voice from behind him, in a clipped, authoritative tone. 'You nearly scored a try there but this little rugger match is over. We're police officers.'

Chapter Seven

Shaw was hauled to his feet, his arms held behind him in a vice-like grip by a man, with two others facing him. He was thrust towards the other men who applied an equally strong hold to his arms. The grounds were now bathed in light from the house and Shaw saw walk in front of him the man that had seized him; a tall, strong-jawed man in his fifties, with a craggy, resolute expression.

'Ah,' said the man. 'I've just seen your collar.' He clicked his fingers at the men holding Shaw's arms. 'Leave him be, you two. This one's all right as far as we know. Go and see what's happening up at the house.'

The two men jogged away along the back path. The man turned to Shaw and looked him up and down.

'It's Reverend Shaw, I take it?'

'Yes,' said Shaw, brushing snow from the front of his jacket. 'I assume you know that a murder and robbery has been committed and that the attackers may be nearby?'

'Yes sir, we're aware of something like that,' said the man. 'We've got the place surrounded and nobody's getting in or out. We've been watching the place for a while and know who everybody is, more or less. I'm afraid that's why we were a little heavy-handed with you just then. We had no way of knowing which one you were.'

'That is quite all right, Mr…?'

'Gregory. Detective Superintendent James Gregory, Special Branch.'

'Special Branch?' queried Shaw. 'The police organisation charged with protecting important persons, and so on?'

'That's right sir,' said Gregory. 'This looks like a very shady business, which is why we've been sent up from London, and the local police aren't involved. We can go into that in a bit more detail later. Perhaps you'd be good enough to come into the house with me? It's bitter out here.' He gestured for Shaw to walk alongside him along the snow-covered path back to the house.

As they approached the building, Shaw heard a small commotion and saw figures moving by the back door. As they came closer he could see Mrs Burward and Elsie held firmly in the arms of two more of Gregory's men.

'We've found another two, sir, in the bushes,' said one of the detectives. 'One of them was armed.' He held out a revolver, gripping it by the barrel, and offered it to Gregory.

'I'll take that, thank you,' said a voice, as another figure stepped out from the back door. It was the man formerly known as Soames. His cadaverous features looked even more deathly pale in the moonlight, and the corpse-like effect was heightened by the twin streams of congealed blood which ran down the left side of his head. He winced in pain as he touched the wound.

He took the pistol from the detective, checked it, and replaced it in the holster under his morning coat.

'That was a bally stupid thing to do,' he said to Elsie.

'Well don't blame me, it was that servant girl that did it,' said Elsie. 'Consider yourself lucky she didn't do more damage if you ask me. Pulling guns on people like that.'

'I was struck on the head by one of the women, with an ornament, sir,' said the man to Gregory. 'They blind-sided me, stole my revolver and locked me in. Seems as if it was the cook that did it.'

'And nor I don't blame her neither,' said Mrs Burward angrily. 'We had no idea you was the police. You should have told us. And how did you get out of that billiard room, I should like to know?'

'I picked the lock,' said the man. 'I suppose I should be thankful you didn't tie me up as well.'

'As this officer hasn't been polite enough to introduce himself,' said Gregory, 'I'll do it for him. This is Detective Sergeant Henry Carter. As you will now realise, he's been working undercover. My name's Superintendent Gregory, Special Branch. You'll be seeing quite a bit of us so let's try to keep things civil, shall we?'

'Sir,' said Carter curtly. 'I'm sorry to say that King Basil has been murdered. Somebody shot him.'

'Blast,' said Gregory. 'After all this work. The Foreign Office will have my guts for garters.' He shook his head angrily.

'May we go round to the front now, sir?' asked Carter. 'It's not all bad. I think we may have found our culprit.'

'Alright Carter,' said Gregory. 'I hope you have. Lead the way.'

The group made its way around the side of the house. Around the open front door was another pair of detectives; one held Ana and the other held Zorard.

'Recognise these two?' said Gregory to Carter.

'Yes sir,' replied the Detective Sergeant. 'The young woman's the one we need to worry about. You can let Mr Zorard go.'

The detective dropped Zorard's arm. He shook himself haughtily. 'As I said, it is not me that should be held, it is her.' He pointed to Ana.

Ana struggled but the policeman held her firmly. She said something in her native tongue at Zorard, who uttered a single word in reply, which seemed to anger Ana even further.

'Now now, English only, please,' said Gregory, raising his hand. 'I'm not having anything said here that we can't all understand.'

'I am sorry,' said Zorard with a bow towards Gregory. 'Of course, we will speak English in order to assist you as best we can. But as I was saying to this other officer, this woman is the one who stole the jewels, and therefore most likely to have killed His Majesty also.'

'He *lies*,' hissed Ana.

'Thank you, that's enough for now,' said Gregory firmly. 'We'll leave the accusations until later. For now I suggest we all go inside out of the cold where I can start interviewing you separately.'

The detectives began herding the group into the hallway. Just then Shaw heard a familiar voice behind him.

'Lucian, thank goodness you're all right.'

He turned to see Mrs Shaw walking towards him, arm in arm with a woman that after a few moments he recognised as Mrs Marchant. Fraser trotted obediently alongside and barked as he recognised his master.

'Marion, what on earth…?' said Shaw.

They embraced, and then Mrs Shaw pulled back with an embarrassed expression on her face, conscious, guessed Shaw, of being watched by a group of strangers.

'Your wife's had a narrow escape,' said Gregory. 'Two men attempted to abduct her and Mrs Marchant but they and your dog put up quite a fight. My men intercepted them at the gate.'

'I was worried about you,' said Mrs Shaw. 'Peggy and

I came to find you but we saw a man in the lane and…oh, it was horrible.'

She clutched her handkerchief to her mouth and Shaw embraced her again firmly. When she withdrew she was slightly calmer. 'You're all right then?' she asked.

'Quite all right,' replied Shaw. 'We ought to go indoors, it is rather cold out here.'

'She put up a damned good show, Padre,' said Mrs Marchant, striding alongside them as they walked into the house. 'Kept her nerve and got the registration number of their car. Foreigners of some sort, nasty types. Armed as well.' She then raised her voice slightly, speaking in Gregory's direction. 'You there,' she said, 'have your men intercepted the vehicle yet?'

Superintendent Gregory paused on the front step. 'Are you addressing me, madam?'

'Certainly,' said Mrs Marchant. 'You seem to be the one in charge. Have your men caught those assailants yet? We've been kept in one of your motor cars and not told a thing. I needn't remind you my husband knows the Chief Constable.'

'No madam, you needn't,' sighed Gregory, as the group entered the hallway. 'We're all very grateful for you and Mrs Shaw telling us about those men. We've got constables looking out for them on the main road to London, where it's most likely they'll be headed. Now if you'll excuse me, I've got a murder and a major robbery on my hands so if you'll let me get on and do my job, the Chief Constable will be able to rest easy in his bed tonight.'

*

'Why the devil did the king have to live in this godforsaken place?' asked Gregory. He was a Londoner through and through, and preferred the busy streets of the capital and his warm flat in Belsize Park to the icy wastes of East Anglia.

The police doctor, newly arrived from Midchester by motor car, replaced the table-cloth over the king's waxen features. 'If he'd had the sense to live in Belgravia we could have protected him properly,' continued Gregory.

Gregory and Carter stood in the drawing room of The Larches, watching pensively and smoking cigarettes, as the police doctor began replacing instruments into his black Gladstone bag.

'He didn't want protection, did he sir?' said Carter. 'We offered it of course – usual Special Branch procedure for someone of his standing – but he emphatically turned it down in writing. Some nonsense about wanting to be treated like any normal Englishman.'

'I remember seeing that letter,' said Gregory. 'The damned fool. And of course I know why he came out here too – besotted with that sharpshooter woman from the music-hall. What's her name again?'

'Elsie Garnham.'

'That's the one. But why not just set her up in a nice little discreet flat in Mayfair and visit her every Friday like any normal man would do?'

Carter shrugged. 'Wasn't a normal man though, was he, sir? He wanted to marry her. Seemed to be properly in love with her. Can't think why, she's the type to give you a tongue-lashing for not folding your pyjamas properly.'

'Hmm,' mused Gregory, stubbing out the end of his De Reszke cigarette in an ashtray on an occasional table. 'Maybe he liked being ordered around after a life of being fawned over. I suppose he also had his reputation to consider. What with being a king and so on. What do they call it when a royal marries a commoner? A morganatic marriage?'

'Something like that,' said Carter. 'There was no funny business going on between them as far as I could tell. She spent every night in that cottage he got for her nearby, and as far as I know he didn't pay her any visits out of hours.'

'The virgin queen, eh?' said Gregory, with a wry smile.

'That could have been the impression she wanted to give him,' said Carter. 'But she's been round the block a few times, has our queen-in-waiting.' He consulted a buff manilla file, one of several on the table beside him. 'Never married, but quite a few boy-friends, from what we can tell. Had up for assault and battery in 1928, broke a chorus girl's nose in a disturbance at a theatre in Ipswich.'

'Sounds a regular hell-cat,' said Gregory. He turned round as he heard the doctor clearing his throat.

'All done, doctor?' asked Gregory.

'We'll know more after the post-mortem,' said the doctor, snapping his bag shut. He smoothed his thinning hair back over his gleaming scalp and adjusted the thick spectacles on his ruddy nose.

'He's been dead about two hours I'd say,' continued the medical man. 'Cause of death, from what I can see without opening him up properly, was myocardial infarction, probably caused by massive trauma to the interventricular septum.'

Gregory sighed. 'What's that in layman's terms?'

'In short,' said the doctor, 'he was shot through the heart.'

'Any idea what sort of gun?' asked Carter.

'Small calibre, I'd say, from the cleanness of the wound,' replied the doctor. 'Unlikely to be anything bigger than point three-eight or we'd be picking bits of him off the carpet. During the war I saw a few poor blighters who copped a packet from those Jerry point four-five Mausers. Some of them had their entire…'

Gregory interrupted him. 'Yes, thank you doctor, we'll leave the war stories for now. Any idea what type of gun or the range?'

'Hard to tell,' said the doctor, a little sullenly after being rebuked. 'My guess would be a rifle from about twenty yards away, but I'm a doctor of medicine, not ballistics.'

'Alright, doctor, thank you, you can take him away now. Drop your report off as soon as possible, won't you?'

The doctor nodded, and two other detectives by the door rolled the body of the king onto a stretcher, covered it with a blanket and lifted it, grunting with the effort of raising the dead man's heavy body.

'Oh and before you go, doctor,' said Gregory, 'I don't want anyone knowing about this. This is all comes under the Official Secrets Act. The last thing we want is any of this getting out to the press.'

'I'll book him in to the mortuary as A.N. Other,' said the doctor. 'First time I've had a royal customer,' he added. 'Any special protocol I ought to observe?'

'Don't worry about that for now,' said Gregory, who was not sure whether the man was joking or not. 'I've got all that to go through with the Foreign Office once we've finished here. Blasted nuisance, it's bad enough having to mop up a normal murder, let alone a royal one.'

'Rather you than me,' said the doctor cheerfully. 'Be seeing you.' He ushered the detectives forward with the stretcher and they disappeared into the corridor.

'What have we got so far, Carter?' asked Gregory, taking another cigarette from a silver case and lighting it after tapping it several times on the case.

'If the doctor's right and he was shot from outside with a rifle,' said Carter, 'the most likely explanation is someone shot him from the gun room opposite. There was a hunting rifle there, I know because I put it back there after the shoot.'

'Shoot?' said Gregory, raising his eyebrows.

'Clay pigeon shoot this afternoon. The king put on a sort of tea party for the parson to talk about his wedding.'

'I see. And there was definitely a rifle in that room?'

'Don't I know it. Her Royal Highness – Miss Garnham – gave me a telling off because I gave it to her thinking it was a shotgun.'

'And where were you when the king got shot?'

'Down in the kitchen. I got another dressing down, from Mrs Burward this time, because I'd used the wrong blasted pot for the tea, and had to go back to the kitchen to get the right one.'

Gregory laughed. 'Remind me why we put you undercover on this one. I thought you used to be a butler?'

'No sir,' said Carter. 'I was an officer's batman during the war, that's all. If you recall it was you who noticed that on my record and came up with the idea of me being sent as an agency butler to keep an eye on the place.'

'I do recall, thank you Carter,' said Gregory. 'But I would have thought you'd know what a teapot was.'

'We didn't have much time for social niceties in the front line,' said Carter. 'My colonel was lucky to have his tea served in a mess tin.'

'Alright Carter, I'm sure you did your best. I couldn't risk keeping a proper guard on this place since the king was adamant he didn't want one. It's just a blasted shame you weren't here to see what happened. You must have heard the shot though.'

'I did,' replied Carter, 'and my first thought was the Bolshies had got him, just like the military intelligence boys – the ones nobody's supposed to know about – warned they might. So I did a recce of the grounds, saw the king through the window lying on the floor, and decided to telephone for help. But the line had been cut so I had to go to the garage. I knew there was another line in there and sure enough, whoever cut the main line didn't bother with that one.'

'Right,' said Gregory, inhaling deeply on his cigarette and blowing out a plume of smoke. 'And it's a good job the military intelligence chaps warned Special Branch to be in the area a short drive away. If we hadn't been, you'd have had to have make do with the local bobbies and God knows what a mess they might have made of things.'

He shivered slightly; the room was icily cold due to the broken window, but it was also a shiver of distaste at the thought of unarmed local policemen attempting to tackle highly trained professional killers.

'Yes sir,' said Carter. 'I then tried to gain access clandestinely to the house, with the intention of keeping everyone inside under guard until reinforcements arrived. That's why I asked you to surround the house but do nothing until my signal.'

'Yes, I didn't quite see the point of that, but you were most insistent on the telephone,' said Gregory. He stubbed out his cigarette in the ashtray. 'Why was that?'

'I've had my suspicions about one or two of the people here for a while, sir,' said Carter. 'I wanted to keep an eye on them, while still acting undercover, in order to see if I could draw them out. I spun them a yarn about seeing intruders in the grounds to help things along.'

'I see,' said Gregory. 'Well it seems obvious what happened. Those two Reds must have killed the king.'

'Two Reds, sir?' asked Carter, with a confused expression on his face.

'Of course, you wouldn't know,' said Gregory. 'A couple of men, foreigners we think, got disturbed by a pair of women in the lane. They made off by motor car but one of the women got the number. Looks likely it was them that shot the king.'

'So that's who those two women were just now,' said Carter. 'One of them was the parson's wife.'

'That's the one. Thanks to her and her pal we shouldn't have too much trouble locating those men. We managed to get through to Ipswich police station on the telephone and they're setting up roadblocks with all available vehicles.'

Carter snorted. 'In a place like Ipswich that will be a pony and trap and two bicycles.'

'Never mind,' said Gregory. 'They're doing their best. Chief Constable's given the order to issue arms as well.'

'That's something I suppose,' said Carter. 'But if you'll forgive me, sir, I still have my suspicions about one or two people closer to home. I think this could have been an inside job.'

Gregory sighed. 'Things are never simple, are they, Carter? All right, let's hear your suspicions then. I read something in one of your reports but forgive me if I can't recall it verbatim.' He folded his arms and leaned back against the door-frame, trying to keep as far away as he could from the icy breeze blowing through the window.

'I think we can rule out some of them,' said Carter, who leaned forward to leaf through the files on the table. 'Mrs Burward, the housekeeper, has worked here for years, for the previous owner, and seems clean as a whistle.'

'I'm guessing the parson is as well,' said Gregory.

'Shaw? Yes sir. Checks out thoroughly. Been the vicar

here for a few years, and has a good war record in the ACD.'

'Army Chaplains' Department?'

'That's the one sir. Can't see him being involved in anything untoward.'

'What on earth have Special Branch got a file on him for?'

'We haven't, sir. This is just my own notes. I knew Zorard had invited the parson here so I did a little asking around the village pub and so on. We servants talk to each other, you know.'

'Good work,' said Gregory. 'Let's assume he's clean then. Strong as a blasted ox though when I tried to take him down. What they call muscular Christianity, I suppose.' Gregory chuckled but Carter's face remained impassive as he leafed through a manilla file.

'There is something on him though,' said Carter, frowning as he turned a page in a file. 'Got mixed up in a murder earlier this year. One of the locals mentioned it so I did a little digging at Records on my afternoon off.'

Gregory snapped his fingers. 'I knew I'd seen him somewhere before. Had his picture in the *Times* or something a few months ago.'

'He would have done,' replied Carter. 'Caused a bit of a stir around here. He attempted to make a citizen's arrest on the chief suspect in a murder case, and nearly got knifed for his trouble.'

'Hmm,' mused Gregory. 'I think we can rule out any funny business from him. He might even be someone we can use to our advantage. What about this Zorard chap?'

'The private secretary? Bit of a mystery I'm afraid. Military intelligence doesn't have anything on him, and now that the Reds have taken over in Fenekslavia there's been no success in finding out anything from them either.

He did fight on the German side in the war though.'

'So did about a million other men, most of them didn't have any choice,' said Gregory. 'I think Fenekslavia was one of those little countries dragged into the war because of that business with Archduke Ferdinand in 1914. It doesn't mean he had any great love for the Huns.'

'I suppose you're right, sir,' mused Carter. 'From what we can tell, Zorard was nothing other than a very loyal servant of the crown.'

'He was saying something about one of the servants though, when we came round the front of the house,' said Gregory. 'What was all that about? Sounded like an accusation. Let's bring him in.'

'Begging your pardon sir, but I haven't mentioned my other suspect,' said Carter. 'The cook.'

'Which one's she?' asked Gregory.

'Young, pretty one with dark hair.'

'Ah, I noticed her. Then again, who wouldn't? Quite a smasher. What's the gen on her?'

'She's one to watch, if you ask me sir. She's a Fenekslavian.'

'Came over with the king and Zorard, presumably?'

'That's just it sir, she didn't. She's a naturalised British subject, married to a local man.'

'I remember that now from your last report. Can't be many like her around. Anything on her?'

'Not a thing sir. I tried the War Office fellows but came up with the same problem as Zorard. They haven't been able to get any intelligence out of Fenekslavia since the uprising.'

'What's her name?'

'Walters sir. Ana Walters.'

Gregory stood up and began pacing the room. 'Then that must be her husband that we picked up earlier.'

'Picked up, sir?'

'Yes, two of the lads at the gate intercepted a man walking into the grounds earlier, thinking he might be one of the Bolshies we'd been warned about. Said he was looking for his wife. Cut up a bit rough and wouldn't come quietly, so I told them to keep him in the van in the lane.'

'That'll be him,' said Carter, nodding. 'Keir Walters. And here's the clincher. He's a Red. Got pinched in the General Strike for assaulting a police constable.'

'What?' exclaimed Gregory. 'Is his wife one as well?'

'Can't say for sure, but my money's on her being involved somehow. She and her husband run some sort of tea shop for socialists. Walters' father owns it, and he's a crank too.' Carter consulted one of the files. 'Bound over twice for affray during pacifist demonstrations.'

'Fighting for peace, eh?' said Gregory with a wry chuckle. 'But how on earth did they let the girl work here?'

'She just turned up out of nowhere, according to Mrs Burward. The king apparently took a liking to her and offered her a job.'

'Seems like old King Basil had an eye for the ladies,' mused Gregory.

'Not just that,' said Carter. 'He missed his home cooking and wanted someone to make his goulash or whatever it is these people eat. Mrs Burward was short-handed in the kitchen and eventually Zorard relented.'

'Ye gods, it's like inviting a wolf into a field of lambs,' said Gregory in disbelief. He stopped pacing and faced Carter. 'Why did you let this happen? You were supposed to be undertaking covert close protection.'

Carter bridled. 'What could I do sir? I expressed my concerns to Zorard but other than that, I had no say in who worked in the house. Zorard paid a visit to their café in

Midchester and when he came back he seemed all right about giving Ana the job, so what was I to do? All I could do was keep an eye on her to see if I could flush her out.'

'Alright, alright Carter,' said Gregory, making a placatory gesture with his hand towards his colleague. 'You did your best I'm sure. Let's get Zorard in and hear what he has to say for himself. Then we'll move on to questioning the others.'

Gregory sighed and looked at his watch. It was going to be a long night, he realised. 'There's something I'd like to get straight before we start asking questions,' he said. He walked to the window and looked out. 'We're surmising that the king was shot from about twenty yards away.'

'Up to twenty yards,' corrected Carter.

'Up to,' agreed Gregory. 'Window broken in here and in the room opposite.' He looked at the snow on the courtyard outside. 'No footprints either. The doctor said the shot probably came from a rifle, and you say there was one in that room.'

'That's right, sir.'

'And who do we know who's a crack shot with a rifle and a reputation for violence?'

'Elsie Garnham. But why would she shoot the man she was just about to marry?'

'You tell me, Sergeant Carter,' replied Gregory with a sigh. He shivered in the cold air by the window and looked with distaste at the stark, leafless trees silhouetted against the moonlight. He braced himself up and turned to face Carter. 'Only one thing for it. Some good old fashioned questioning.'

Chapter Eight

A few miles away, Sergeant Harry Onslow and PC Fred Mills of the Ipswich police shivered as they sat in their brand-new Wolseley 'Straight Eight' squad car, parked discretely in a lane off the main arterial road between Norwich and London. The car, the pride of the city force's small motor pool, was unheated and bitterly cold inside. Onslow was a stickler for regulations and had just told Mills to remove his non-uniform scarf.

'Suppose somebody grabs on that and pulls it,' said Onslow. 'That's why you can't wear one.'

'I'm more likely to freeze to death than be strangled just now, sarge,' said Mills, petulantly.

'It's sergeant, not "sarge"', corrected Onslow. He began to unwrap a sandwich from some grease-proof paper.

'Sorry, ser…geant,' replied Mills. He was just 22 and had only been on the force a year or so. He pulled at the tight canvas webbing of the holster belt around his waist.

The holster contained the heavy Webley revolver issued to him a short time ago after a quick thinking member of Gregory's Special Branch team had telephoned from a call box to Ipswich police station, where an equally quick-thinking Inspector had managed to telephone the

Chief Constable at home, who had then rapidly organised as many men and motor cars as he could spare, issued them with firearms and placed them on three main roads.

'Can I take this thing off, sergeant?' asked Mills, pointing to the belt. 'It's digging into me something awful.'

'No you may not,' replied Onslow. 'The Superintendent said those men we're to look out for are armed and dangerous. You need that pistol where you can reach it.'

'What are they supposed to have done, these men?' asked Mills.

'Armed robbery, is all I got told. It must be that as they don't issue revolvers for no good reason,' said Onslow. 'You just keep your eyes on that road.'

'You ever shot anyone, sergeant?'

'Not as a copper, no.'

'In the war then?' Mills asked with the enthusiasm of one too young to have seen combat.

'Yes.'

'A Jerry?'

'No, a Turk. I was in the Dardanelles, not France.'

'What you shoot him for?'

'For asking damned silly questions.'

Onslow bit into his sandwich and chewed silently, indicating that the discussion was closed. Mills took the hint. He hugged his arms close to his chest for warmth and stared out of the windscreen into the darkness. A car's headlights appeared from the bend in the road. In the instant it passed under a flickering oil-lit street light, he noticed the start of the licence number.

'What was the number of the car again?' asked Mills urgently.

'Eh?'

'The car, the number of the car we're looking for.'

'All right lad, keep your hair on.' Onslow put down his sandwich and consulted his notebook. 'BJ 193 or possibly 198. Dark-coloured Morris Cowley or similar. Witness said it had a dickey seat at the back.'

'That was it, sergeant. Just passed by. BJ something anyway.'

'Well don't just sit there lad, get moving.'

'The Super said we're to telephone if…'

'We haven't got time to jump out and telephone the blasted station. He'll be halfway to London by now. Get moving.'

Mills, his heart pounding, needed no further encouragement. Within seconds he had pulled out onto the slush-covered main road and was accelerating rapidly. The Wolseley's large engine gave out a satisfying roar, but with an indication of greater power held in reserve. Onslow leaned forward to the dashboard and turned on the Winkworth bell, which rang out in the frosty air with a shrill, repetitive insistence.

'I can see his tail-light up ahead,' said Onslow. 'Keep on him, there's no turnings off this section for another half mile or so.'

A few moments later the squad car had caught up easily with the little Morris. Mills flashed his headlamps to indicate that the driver should halt, but instead, the small car surged ahead.

'That's them all right,' said Onslow, as the headlamps illuminated the interior of the car. 'Two men, heavy set. Foreigners apparently.' He pulled his revolver from its holster, checked the chamber and replaced it.

'Remember your training, son,' said Onslow. 'Pull alongside and force him over. If he won't move, get in front of him and block him.'

'Righto,' said Mills, gripping the steering wheel.

'Ruddy snow,' he added, as the car skidded slightly on a bend. A lorry passed slowly in the opposite direction, but the traffic was fortunately light, most drivers presumably not risking travel on the dark, icy roads. Seeing a clear stretch ahead, Mills accelerated and pulled alongside the car.

Onslow opened his window and jerked his index finger several times in a 'pull over' gesture. The other car maintained its speed, its occupants hidden from view within the darkened interior.

'Blasted idiot's not having it,' said Onslow. The car decelerated momentarily as Mills eased off on the accelerator.

'Something up ahead sergeant,' said Mills. 'Have to pull back.'

'Get him again as quick as you can,' urged Onslow. 'We might lose him in town if he gets there.'

Once the oncoming vehicle had passed, Mills accelerated again and overtook the Morris easily, slowing down to force the little car to follow suit.

There was a loud crash as the rear window and windscreen of the police car shattered; Mills wrestled with the steering wheel as he struggled to retain control of the vehicle on a patch of ice. He squinted against the blast of icy air roaring through the space where seconds before there had been glass.

'They're shooting sarge,' he yelled. 'What do we do now? Sarge?'

No reply came from Onslow, who was slumped forward in his seat, blood oozing from a wound on the side of his head.

Mills looked in the rear view mirror and saw the Morris two hundred yards behind, attempting a three point turn in the road. He brought the Wolseley to a rapid halt and touched Onslow's shoulder.

'Sergeant?'

Onslow moaned and turned his head towards Mills. He managed to speak, albeit in a low whisper.

'Alright,' he said. 'Bullet scraped my ear I think. Must have passed just by me. Can't hear a blasted thing.'

'What do I do now?' asked Mills desperately.

'Get…the blighters…'

Onslow became silent as he fell into a faint.

Mills took a deep breath and turned the car in the road. Its transmission barked a discordant complaint as he attempted to double-declutch too quickly. A few moments later the car was facing the opposite direction and Mills saw the tail-light of the Morris retreating into the darkened distance.

Mills gunned the engine the car leaped forward. He no longer noticed the freezing cold air on his face as the vehicle reached forty miles an hour within seconds.

The snow was worse on this side of the road, realised Mills, as the car skidded momentarily. Up ahead, he saw the little Morris swerve sideways on, then come to a halt as its front wheels became trapped in the ditch by the side of the road.

Twenty yards behind, Mills stopped the Wolseley. After checking that Onslow was still breathing, he exited the car and edged forward under the cover of the foliage by the side of the road, feeling snow slip down over the top of his boots as his feet sank into the deep drifts in the ditch.

Mills fumbled with the buckle on his webbing holster and pulled his revolver out, momentarily getting his hand caught up in the lanyard that secured the weapon to his tunic. He had only signed up for firearms training as a lark, never expecting to have to use a gun, but now he desperately tried to remember what he was supposed to do with it.

He raised the pistol and pointed it at the car, which was illuminated by the faint glow from the headlamps of his own vehicle. Swallowing hard to ensure his voice did not crack, he called out.

'Get out of the car.'

The driver's door opened and a heavy-set man in an overcoat, with his hat pulled down over his eyes, got out. His hands were raised and Mills could see that one of them was wrapped in a blood-soaked piece of cloth.

'And the other side,' shouted Mills.

The passenger door opened slightly and a booted foot emerged, and then stopped.

'Come on,' called Mills. 'Don't mess me about. We've got reinforcements on the way.'

The door opened fully and in an instant, a figure emerged; there was a flash of light and an explosion, then a tinkling of glass as a bullet struck one of the Wolseley's headlamps.

Mills dropped to one knee and fired. The pistol bucked in his hand with a heavy recoil as the rear window of the Morris shattered. The man in the car fired a second time, and Mills heard the whine of a bullet travel close by his ear. He saw the other man, the driver, edge toward him.

Mills fired again and this time, the bullet hit its target. The passenger had no chance against the heavy Webley revolver, famous for its stopping power. He slumped forward, the pistol tumbling out of his limp hand into the road.

'Don't you move!' shouted Mills at the driver, who was now only a few feet away. Mills stood up and repeated the order, but the man kept on moving, as if he didn't understand what was being said. The man made a dive for his accomplice's gun, clearly visible against the whiteness of the snowy road.

Mills felt his heart sink, but before he had time to feel fear, he fired again. There was no possibility of a miss at this range, and the driver collapsed in the road with his outstretched arm just inches from the pistol. His hand twitched twice, and then was still.

*

'I'll try not to keep you too long, sir,' said Superintendent Gregory as Shaw was shown into the drawing room by Sergeant Carter. 'I've sent your wife and Mrs Marchant home in their motor car, with one of my men driving it. They've had quite a shock, but they seem a tough pair. Parker will stay with them at the vicarage until we drop you off as well.'

'That is most kind of you,' said Shaw, standing rather awkwardly in the drawing room. He looked down at the carpet to avoid standing where the king's body had lain.

'He's been removed, sir,' said Gregory. 'We've had a thorough check of the room as well, so please, sit down, won't you?'

Gregory gestured to an arm-chair as Carter shut the door of the drawing room. Shaw half sat, half collapsed into a deep leather armchair.

'Must have been quite a shock for you,' said Gregory. He took out his cigarette case and offered it to Shaw.

'No thank you,' said Shaw. 'But I wonder if…?' He took out his pipe and showed it to the detective.

'Of course, sir, of course,' said Gregory. 'Nothing better to calm the nerves, eh?'

Once the two men had both lit their respective smoking materials, Gregory perched on the arm of a chair opposite Shaw.

'Now if you don't mind sir, I'd like you to describe exactly what happened when the king got shot.'

'We were all seated around the fire,' said Shaw. 'I was in the same chair that I am in now.'

'And where was the king?' asked Gregory.

'He was opposite me. Miss Garnham was on his left, and Mr Zorard on his right.

'And the servants?'

'Mrs Burward was by the door, as was Soames.'

'And they were all here when the king was shot?'

'No, not all. Soames and Miss Garnham had left before then. Soames to fetch more tea, and Miss Garnham to...' Shaw paused and puffed on his pipe, unsure of how to proceed.

'To do what, sir?' prompted Gregory.

'There had been something of an argument,' said Shaw, 'and Miss Garnham left the room in rather an angry state, it seemed.'

'I see,' said Gregory. He took a puff on his cigarette and tapped it over the ashtray on the tea-table. 'Then what happened?'

'A few moments later Mr Zorard told everyone to be quiet. He said he had heard someone outside.'

'Did you hear anything?'

'I must confess I did not. But Mr Zorard told us all to remain quiet. He went to the window to look out, then opened it slightly to listen.'

'And what then?'

'That was when the rock was thrown through the window.'

'Rock? What rock?'

Shaw leaned forward and pointed with his pipe stem to the rock on the tea table. 'That one.'

'I wondered what that thing was doing there,' said Gregory. 'I thought it must be some foreign ornament.'

'No, I saw it come through the window and land somewhere on the floor.'

'Did anyone pick it up?'

'Not then. It was just after that the shot was fired, and the king collapsed. He died a few moments later.'

'Where would you say the shot came from?'

Shaw paused. 'From the direction of the window.'

'Yes, but how far away? Was it a distant sound, or could it have come from just outside the window?'

'I don't follow, Superintendent.'

'We've reason to believe the king was shot with a rifle, but we don't know where from. It could have been in the room opposite, or by someone standing in the courtyard.'

'I see,' said Shaw. 'Without hearing shots fired from both locations as a comparison, it is difficult to say. At a guess I would say it was from the courtyard.'

'Did you see anybody through the window?'

'No. It was pitch black in the room as well as outside, once Mr Zorard switched off the lamp, and my eyes did not have time to adjust.'

'Very well,' said Gregory. 'Now, about this rock. Who put it on the table?'

'I did, Superintendent. It had a note attached to it.'

'Good Lord,' said Gregory. He seemed genuinely surprised, although Shaw noticed that Carter's face remained impassive.

'Where is the note?' asked Gregory.

'I believe Mr Zorard put it in his pocket,' replied Shaw.

'Any idea what it said?'

'Yes, it was a demand for the crown jewels of Fenekslavia to be put on the front step, or there would be more killing.'

'Written in English, I assume?'

'In Fenekslavian and English.'

'You definitely saw it?'

'Certainly. I could not, of course, understand the Fenekslavian text, but the English writing was clear enough.'

Gregory turned to Carter. 'That explains what all that fuss at the door with Zorard and that servant was about. He was saying something about her taking the jewels.'

'Sir,' said Carter, 'perhaps we ought to discuss that after you have finished interviewing Mr Shaw.'

Gregory stubbed out his cigarette and cleared his throat. 'I hope you don't think, Mr Shaw, that Detective Sergeant Carter is implying that you had anything to do with this.'

'Of course not, Superintendent,' said Shaw. 'It is quite understandable that certain things should not be discussed in my hearing. If I may continue, however, there is something further of interest you may like to hear.'

Shaw outlined the events following the king's death and then took the small cartridge case from his waistcoat pocket. Gregory examined it closely.

'I found this near the back step where somebody shot at Mr Zorard,' said Shaw. 'From the patterns in the snow around it, it looked as if somebody had been trying to find it, but failed.'

'Put it in an envelope, please, sergeant,' said Gregory to Carter, who took the bullet and placed it in a small brown envelope which he took out of his pocket.

'Were you with Zorard when he was shot at?' continued Gregory.

'No, I only heard the shots. Someone fired at him from both the front and back of the house.'

'Anyone else there at the time?'

'Yes – I was with Mrs Walters and Mrs Burward,' said Shaw. 'We were all waiting in the hall.'

'Where was Miss Garnham during all this?'

'We did not find her until later. She was in the vicinity of the billiard room.'

'I see,' mused Gregory. 'Well, that cartridge could be a useful piece of evidence. I won't question you any further sir – for now – but you've been very helpful.'

Gregory stood up and Shaw followed suit, taking this as his cue to leave.

'I would offer you a lift home, but unfortunately I can't spare the men,' said Gregory.

'That is quite understandable,' replied Shaw. 'I shall be quite alright on my bicycle.'

'Right you are then,' said Gregory. 'Carter will show you to the gate.' Gregory then pulled himself up to his full height, an inch or so shorter than Shaw. 'I must remind you before you go, sir,' he said, adopting a more formal tone, 'that this is all to remain absolutely confidential. This could be a matter of national security and you are not to discuss it with anyone.'

'I understand, Superintendent,' replied Shaw. 'Would I be permitted to talk about the night's events, however, with my wife? She has had rather a shock and I find it can be quite beneficial to discuss one's concerns after a traumatic experience.'

'I'd rather you didn't,' said Gregory, 'but since she's had a certain amount of involvement herself I suppose it won't do too much harm.'

'Thank you, Superintendent,' said Shaw. Carter opened the door and Shaw walked over to the doorway.

'I wouldn't worry too much, sir,' said Gregory. 'My money's on the culprits being those two your wife and her friend scared off. Once we've got them we should be able to find the jewels as well.'

'Oh, there is one more thing,' said Shaw. 'You know, of course, that the crown jewels are paste?'

'Paste?' asked Gregory, in a puzzled tone.

'Replicas,' said Shaw. 'Forgive me, it has been rather a trying day and I forgot to mention it. Mr Zorard informed me the real jewels are kept in a safety deposit box in London.' Shaw noticed a look of surprise cross Carter's face.

'That's most interesting, Mr Shaw,' said Gregory. He looked at Carter. 'Then why on earth was that Zorard fellow so worked up just now about them being stolen by the cook?'

Carter cleared his throat and Shaw saw the sergeant's eyes flick towards him. Gregory appeared to take the hint and extended his hand to Shaw.

'Well, thank you again sir,' he said. 'We'll be in touch again but for now, as I mentioned, this must all remain strictly confidential.'

Shaw stepped out of the room and a few minutes later, he was riding home slowly and cautiously along the lane back to Lower Addenham, his little bicycle lamp forming a tiny pool of light amid the icy blackness of the midwinter night, like some strange luminous sea-creature moving through the depths of a bottomless ocean.

*

'I have already spoken to your men outside,' said Zorard, as he was shown into the drawing room by Carter. 'Is an interrogation really necessary?'

'Nobody's interrogating you, Mr Zorard,' said Gregory. 'We just want to ask you a few questions. We'll be as brief as we can.'

Zorard looked around the room. 'Where has His Majesty been taken?'

Gregory paused. 'To a hospital, sir,'

'You mean a mortuary?'

'A hospital mortuary, yes.'

Gregory shook his head. 'He should be lying in state. But I suppose it is a necessary procedure in such a case.'

'I'm afraid so, sir,' said Gregory. 'Won't you sit down?' He gestured to an armchair.

Zorard sat down and took out his cigarette case. 'May I?'

'Of course,' said Gregory. Zorard lit a fat, oval cigarette and soon the room was filled with the harsh aroma of Balkan tobacco.

'I should have thought you have all the information you need, from this informer,' said Zorard, pointing with his cigarette to Carter. The sergeant gazed at Zorard impassively from his post by the door.

'Detective Sergeant Carter is a Special Branch officer sir, he is not an informer,' replied Gregory. 'He was placed here on covert operations because we received intelligence that an attempt might be made on the king's life.'

'He did not do a very good job,' said Zorard. 'Either as a secret policeman or a butler. I would have preferred it if I had been informed of the secret operation. As far as I knew, Soames was a genuine butler sent by an agency, not a spy.'

Carter bridled at the remark and was about to speak but Gregory cut him off.

'We might have been able to protect His Majesty had we been allowed to give close protection,' said the Superintendent firmly. 'Unfortunately we had to resort to subterfuge with just one man in place which was not ideal.'

'No it was not,' replied Zorard. 'But His Majesty was insistent that no bodyguards should be in the house. He wanted no fuss.'

'Yes, we have a copy of the letter sent to the Home Office,' said Gregory. 'At any rate, that's in the past and there's nothing we can do about it now. My task is to find out who killed the king and why, and to find those jewels.'

'A simple enough case,' said Zorard. 'The king was killed by Bolshevik agents, most likely aided by the woman who calls herself Mrs Ana Walters.'

'We've taken due note of your allegations,' said Gregory, 'but first I'd like to hear your account of what happened.' Gregory sat down in an armchair facing Zorard. He took out his cigarette case and lit a De Reske; Carter took out a notebook and began writing.

'Very well,' said Zorard. 'During the serving of the afternoon tea, I heard a noise outside the window.'

'What time was this?' asked Gregory.

'About half past four.'

'And what sort of sound was it?'

'That of movement outside. Boots scraping, perhaps.'

'And you believed it to be assassins?'

'I was not sure. You will know, of course, that the Bolsheviks have issued a pardon to His Majesty, Inspector.'

'Yes, we're aware of that. And it's Superintendent.'

'My apologies. The English ranks, I still find them confusing.'

'Never mind. Go on.'

'I told the others to remain quiet and still, while I looked through the window.'

'Did you open it?'

'A small amount. Sufficient to hear anyone outside, but not enough to allow a person to force entry.'

'Did you see anyone?'

'Not until after the rock was thrown.'

'So somebody threw a rock, and then you saw him?'

'For just a moment. A figure opposite the window.'

'How far away?'

'On the other side of the courtyard. About five metres.'

'What's that in English?'

Carter interjected. 'About fifteen feet, sir.'

'Right,' continued Gregory. 'Was it a man or a woman?'

'It was too dark to tell,' said Zorard, 'and light was reflected on the window. I switched off the table lamp and returned to the window. That was when the shot was fired.'

'You are a military man, I think, sir?'

'Of course,' replied Zorard. 'I have served many years. First in the Engineers and then the Royal Guard. Why?'

'Because I'm hoping you'll know a bit about assessing where shots have come from when somebody starts shooting.'

'Certainly,' replied Zorard. He leaned forward to stub out his cigarette and looked Gregory in the eye. 'It is the basic training of an officer in the field to locate the direction of fire. I believe the shot most probably came from the gun room opposite.'

'Mr Shaw says that later on, you were fired at by a person or persons unknown, when you tried to leave the house. Can you tell us a bit about that?'

'My intention was to summon assistance using the telephone in the garage. But when I attempted to leave the house, I was shot at, when I was at both the front and back doors.'

'Did you see who did it?'

'No. I had not time. I fell to the ground on both occasions for cover, and then crawled back inside the house.'

'Pistol or rifle shots?'

'I am not sure.'

'But as a military man, you could hazard a guess?'

'"Hazard a guess?" Ah, you mean make a guess. Yes, I would say, a pistol, because of the nearness of the sound.'

'How near?'

'At the front door, from quite far off. Perhaps from the bushes on the drive. At the back door, much closer. About four…let me see, about 12 of your English feet away.'

'And yet you didn't see anyone?'

'The shot came from the direction of the bushes by the door. Whoever fired must have been concealed within them.'

'Do you own a pistol?'

Zorard smiled again. 'I brought one with me, Superintendent. It was necessary to have one in my possession to protect the king when we left Fenekslavia.'

'Do you carry it around with you?'

'No, it was explained to me by your Home Office men when we arrived in Dover that pistols may not be carried in England, and so I handed it over to them. I have the receipt if you wish to check.'

'That won't be necessary at this stage, sir,' said Gregory. 'Are there any other guns in the house?'

'Only the sporting guns in the room opposite this.'

'Very well,' said Gregory, leaning forward in his chair.

'Now, about this accusation you made towards the cook. Care to tell us about that?'

'You will forgive my earlier anger, Superintendent. I was not myself, you will understand, due to the shock of the king's death. I can relate matters to you more calmly now.'

'Go on.'

'I had my suspicions about Mrs Ana Walters from the beginning. She arrived unannounced and offered her services to the king as a cook. I attempted to send her away, but His Majesty was insistent she should be offered a position.'

'Why do you think that was?'

'I believe one should not…how is the saying…speak ill of the dead.'

'You mean his two main interests in life were chasing women and stuffing his face, and she scored on both counts,' said Carter.

Zorard winced. 'Superintendent, must I suffer these insults to the memory of my sovereign?'

'Yes, all right, thank you Carter, that's enough,' said Gregory, glaring at the sergeant. 'Suffice to say Mrs Walters was given a post here. Against your better judgement.'

'Of course. My suspicions were confirmed when I visited Mrs Walters' caféteria in Midchester and found it to be stocked with revolutionary pamphlets.'

'Yet you still gave her the job?'

'Not of my own will. His Majesty ordered it. Fenekslavia is an absolute monarchy, Superintendent. One does not contradict the king. I decided instead to keep careful watch on Mrs Walters, and I was proved right.'

'What do you mean by that?'

'I left the crown jewels of Fenekslavia on the front step,

just as the assassins ordered. And she took them.'

Gregory stared at Zorard suspiciously. 'You gave them up just like that? You didn't even put up a fight?'

'Why should I?' asked Zorard. 'They were imitations.'

'Fakes?'

'Yes. Worn for ceremonial occasions and so on. But convincing enough, I thought, to give the assassins what they wanted and to get rid of them before any further bloodshed took place.'

'I see. And where are the real jewels?'

'In a safe deposit box in London.'

'Where exactly, sir, if you don't mind my asking?'

'In the Ritz Hotel. I sometimes accompanied His Majesty there and arranged for a box for any valuable items he might buy on his London trips. We stopped there before coming to this house. One must be careful of thieves, even in England.'

'We'll have to check that box.'

'Of course. I will be happy to accompany your officers there myself.'

'All right. We'll let you know. So you put these paste jewels on the step and what then?'

'I called out that the jewels were ready to be taken.'

'What then?'

'I saw a figure approach and closed the door quickly, in case I should be shot at again. I watched, however, through the small window by the door. I saw someone take the bag of jewels and walk away along the drive.'

'Did you recognise that person?'

'Yes, it was the one known as Ana Walters.'

'If you don't mind, sir,' interrupted Carter.

'Yes, what is it?' asked Gregory in a slightly annoyed tone.

'What language did you call out in?' asked the

sergeant. 'English, or Fenekslavian?'

'Fenekslavian,' replied Zorard, looking with distaste at Carter.

'Alright sir, thank you very much,' said Gregory, standing up. 'I think that will be all for now. You're free to go – but we'll need you for further questioning so don't leave the country, will you?'

'And what of the king's funeral, the arrangements, the succession?' said Zorard.

'You'll have to sit tight on that for a while I'm afraid,' said Gregory. 'Matter of national security. You're not to talk to anybody about this until I've had clearance from the Home Office.'

'But this is preposterous,' spluttered Zorard. 'The king cannot be left on some slab in some mortuary! There are arrangements to be made. I shall speak to your superiors.'

'Now then, Mr Zorard,' sighed Gregory. 'There's no need to take on. I'll let you into a little secret. We've got good reason to believe there are at least two foreign agents at large, quite possibly linked to the death of the king.'

Zorard spoke in a calmer tone. 'It is as I feared, of course. I did not believe the Bolsheviks when they issued their pardon. Of course, it must be kept secret until you have apprehended these men.'

'I'm glad you understand sir,' said Gregory. 'That'll be all for now. You can go to your quarters while we finish up here.'

After Zorard had left, Carter turned to Gregory with an eager look. 'That ties in with what Detective Constable Tillotson said just now while we were waiting, sir. He was on the detail watching the front of the house and heard a man talking in some sort of foreign language, then a few moments later they nabbed the girl on the drive after I'd given the signal.'

'Yes,' said Gregory, as he rubbed his chin. 'But the girl didn't have the jewels on her, did she?'

'No, but like Zorard said, she could have ditched them in the bushes. Come daylight we'll be able to have a proper search.'

'All very well, unless she somehow got them to an accomplice.'

'Not likely though, is it sir? Not with our men watching the house.'

'Didn't Tillotson see the girl taking the bag?'

Carter's face fell. 'No sir, he only heard them talking foreign to each other.'

'Well why didn't he see anything?' insisted Gregory.

'He was…he had to answer a call of nature, sir. I think it was the cold weather.'

'Good God,' sighed Gregory. 'Tell him to wear a baby's napkin next time he's on duty.'

'Sorry sir. Looks like Walters is our man, though. I mean, our woman.'

'Could well be,' said Gregory, as he looked into the distance beyond the broken window pane. 'Could well be. But the doctor reckons it was a rifle shot, and so does Zorard. If it was, it could have come from the gun room. And who do we know who's a crack shot with a rifle who was out of this room at the time?'

'Elsie Garnham,' replied Carter. 'But honestly sir, she and the king seemed like genuine love-birds, from what I could tell.'

'Never rely on appearances, Carter,' said Gregory, shaking his head. 'You should know that as an undercover man. Let's get Miss Garnham and then Walters and her husband in here, then finish up for the night. And I hope there aren't any men on those roadblocks answering the call of nature when those two agents drive past.'

Chapter Nine

An unshaven man in military uniform wiped his hands across his face, as the snow piled ever higher outside on the window-sill behind him. The makeshift radio room in the former Royal Palace of Kecsprem was unheated, due to fuel shortages.

The man shivered and paced up and down. He had dismissed the other members of the junta, telling them to go home until he was able to give them further information. Now he was alone, apart from the radio operator who sat impassively by his array of instruments, listening for signals, but no sound came through the apparatus except the rising and falling whine of static.

What had happened to Agent A and Agent B? he wondered. He smiled at the initials. One of the committee members had wanted to give them the code names Marx and Engels, but he had over-ruled this, thinking it might annoy the Russians with whom they had to work closely.

He looked at his watch. A and B should have sent a report by now, via a coded message telephoned to the Russian embassy in London, which would then be forwarded by radio to this very room. A thought struck him; perhaps A and B had simply not been able to find a telephone. Then he pushed the thought away; of course there would be telephones everywhere in England. It was not a backward country like Fenekslavia.

He then thought about sending a message via the radio to the Russian embassy. But his contacts in Moscow had expressly forbidden this. Diplomatic relations with Great Britain could not be risked under any circumstances, and they particularly did not want to be associated with the death of a foreign monarch on English soil.

The man continued pacing. He imagined A and B captured, interrogated in an English jail. Or perhaps worse. The British police were not routinely armed, he knew, but he had a feeling that their secret police carried weapons and in a case such as this, such policemen might be brought into play.

He would just have to wait, he thought. Perhaps the report would come tomorrow. If it did not, there was always the contingency plan of the other agent they had sent, known as C, who was acting undercover and might still be able to carry out the plan. The third man.

He corrected himself for such a bourgeois mistake. He felt terribly tired. He remembered, of course, that C was not a man, but a woman.

*

'We'll try to keep this short, Miss Garnham,' said Gregory, as Elsie was shown into the drawing room by Carter. 'Sit down, won't you?' He gestured to an armchair.

Elsie appeared composed, but touched her hair repeatedly in what seemed like a nervous gesture as her eyes flicked around the room.

'I realise this must be very upsetting for you,' said Gregory, 'but there's one or two things I'd like to clear up if you don't mind.'

'That's quite alright, Superintendent,' said Elsie. 'I was beginning to think it was all too good to be true. Like something out of a novel or the pictures.'

'You being engaged to marry a king, you mean?'

'Yes. Silly really, when you think about it. But Basil and I we…well, we loved each other in our own way.'

'I see,' said Gregory. 'I'm not here to pry into your personal life, miss, all I want to know is where you were around the time the king was shot.'

'I was in the billiard room, along the corridor. Gathering my thoughts.'

'I understand you had something of an argument with the king.'

'I wouldn't call it that. A disagreement, perhaps.'

'What was the cause of it?'

'He…he told me he'd given up the idea of going back to Fenekslavia, and that he wanted me to carry on with my act.'

'Your sharp-shooter act, in the theatre?'

'Yes. Well I…it came as a bit of a shock. I suppose every girl dreams of a fairytale wedding, doesn't she?'

'I'll take your word for it, miss.'

'I realised that it was all just a silly dream. I wasn't going to become a queen and I wasn't even going to have a big wedding, just something in an ordinary country church.' Elsie sniffed and then dabbed at her eyes with a handkerchief. 'You must think I'm an awful gold-digger.'

'That's not for me to judge, miss. It's not as if you'd have been living in poverty in a place like this though.' Gregory looked around at the plush furnishings and the large faux-Tudor fireplace of the drawing room.

'It's not a royal palace though, is it?' said Elsie, in a melancholy tone.

'Anyway,' said Gregory, 'to return to the matter in hand, did you hear a shot when you were in the billiard room?'

'No. I heard glass breaking and went out into the corridor. I thought a picture must have fallen off the wall, but then I saw the window of the gun room opposite was shattered.'

'Did you see anyone in the gun room?'

'No, it was too dark really. I could only just make out that the gun room window and its little bits of frame were all broken. I only had a moment to notice it because then I heard a shot.'

Gregory frowned. 'Do you know what a muzzle flash is, Miss Garnham?'

'Of course. I've been around guns most of my life. For all the good it's done me.'

'And did you see a muzzle flash from the gun room window?'

'No. I just heard a shot.'

'From the direction of the gun room window?'

'Hard to tell. That courtyard is a sort of echo chamber.'

'I assume you've fired all sorts of weapons in your…line of work.'

'Yes.'

'Could you say if it was a rifle or a pistol shot?'

'Hard to tell, again. I'd wager a small bore rifle but I couldn't swear to it. When we searched the gun room we found a hunting rifle and a spent cartridge in there.'

Gregory and Carter exchanged glances. 'What did you do after you heard the shot?' continued the Superintendent.

'I…well it sounds awful, but I lost my nerve. I thought something terrible must have happened and I froze with fear. I hid in an alcove and waited until I heard voices along the corridor. That's when I met with Mr Zorard and the others.'

'Sounds a bit odd,' said Carter from the doorway. 'You had plenty of nerve when you were urging the others to shoot their way out of here.'

'That was different,' snapped Elsie. 'I'd seen what had been done to Basil by then and I wasn't going to let them get away with it.'

'Alright, thank you Carter,' admonished Gregory. 'You've been very helpful. Now, Miss Garnham, I understand you have a cottage nearby.'

'Yes, that's right. Basil arranged it for me. He was a gentleman, and didn't think it right for me to live under his roof before the wedding.'

'Very well. I'll arrange for one of the men to escort you over there.' Gregory showed Elsie to the door and then placed his hand on her arm.

'I must remind you miss, that you are not to speak about tonight's events to anyone. This is a matter of national security at the moment and we can't risk the papers hearing about this. Do I make myself clear?'

'Of course,' replied Elsie. 'Matter of fact I don't feel like talking to anybody anyway. I've got my theories about who did this and I dare say you have too, but I'll keep them to myself.'

'I suppose you think Ana Walters is involved?' asked Carter.

'Not for me to say,' said Elsie. 'But it's a bit odd, isn't it? Turning up out of nowhere, and her a Fenekslavian as well.'

'Thank you Miss Garnham,' said Gregory, 'as you say we have our theories, and we'll be talking to Mrs Walters presently. You may also like to know that we've reason to believe foreign agents were involved in this matter.'

Elsie stepped through the doorway and then turned to Gregory. 'I suppose they got away with the jewels…?' she asked.

'I'm not at liberty to say at the moment miss,' said Gregory. 'But thank you again for your co-operation. Sergeant Carter will show you out.'

Moments after Carter and Elsie had left the room, another of Gregory's men put his head around the door.

'Sorry to trouble you sir,' he said, 'Only we've done a search like you said and we found something.'

'Don't keep me in suspense, Lovat,' said Gregory with a bored sigh. 'What is it?'

'We had a look around the kitchens and so on, sir, and the coat-rack by the back door, and in one of the servant's bags we found this.' He held out a pencil, onto which was suspended, from its trigger guard, an automatic pistol. 'There were a few bits of silver cutlery in the bag as well.'

'Whose bag?' asked Gregory, with sudden interest.

'There's a name written on the inside, sir. A. Walters.'

*

That night, Shaw dreamed of the war again. The dream came in different forms but always with the same underlying sense of trepidation. He found himself wandering in an endless maze of trenches, deserted but for rows of corpses stacked like sandbags against the walls. Snow covered everything, although he felt no sense of cold, and the blasted landscape stretched out before him into the distance, merging with a white sky.

I should not be here, he thought to himself, in the manner of one who is beginning to realise that he is in a dream, but cannot yet wake up. I should not be here…the war is over. Then he turned a corner and before him were the faces of soldiers he had ministered to in his chaplaincy days. The faces were grimy and tinged with exhaustion and fear, but looked up at him with expectation and trust.

He suddenly realised where he was; it was Cambrai before the big push in December 1917. Again, Shaw's mind whirled in confusion; how could he be here when the war had been over for 12 years? Had the Armistice all been a dream, and somehow, this was reality? He looked down and saw that, although he wore his chaplain's uniform, his jacket was open, revealing his pyjamas underneath. Self-consciously he pulled his jacket across his body, but the men did not seem to notice.

'Do the honours, Padre,' said a man, a corporal whose face he dimly remembered but whose name he could not recall. A sapper, he thought. One of the contingent of Royal Engineers to which he had been briefly attached.

The man grinned, toothlessly, and pointed with a ragged, gloved hand across the shattered landscape to a tower. Shaw remembered it; there had been a ruined chateau close to the lines, and all that remained of it had been the broken skeleton of a small two storey-tower. This tower, however, was huge and dark, stretching hundreds of feet into the air until it disappeared from view in white mist.

From somewhere came the sound of men singing in low voices; it must be the Welsh Fusiliers up the line, thought Shaw; although he could not make out the words, he recognised the tune: *Good King Wenceslas.*

'We've a Christmas present for that sniper,' whispered the corporal, his face inches from Shaw's. His breath was warm and exuded a stench of decay. 'Been picking us off like blooming pigeons. Well we pigeons is shooting back.'

Shaw heard the whine of bullets from the tower, and several of the men in the trench slumped forward; none of the other men paid any attention to their fallen comrades, but all fixed their hollow eyes on Shaw.

The corporal gave Shaw a box with a lever on the top. 'Us sappers have mined the Hun's nest. Better do it now before he realises.' He nodded towards the battlefield, and Shaw saw lumps of soil mixed with snowflakes trickle slowly from his helmet as he did so. Shaw looked over the parapet of the trench and saw a wire snaking from the box into the distance towards the tower.

The sound of singing grew louder, but this time it was of men drunkenly yelling the words of the Bridges hymn, to the raucous accompaniment of a ragtime piano.

What with care and toil he buildeth
Tower and temple, turn to dust.

'Do us all a favour, Padre,' whispered the corporal. 'Turn it all to dust, eh?'

Suddenly in the depths of his consciousness Shaw remembered the name of the man: Guthrie. Poor, simple, trusting Corporal Guthrie. He had come to Shaw on the eve of the battle, asking in a matter-of-fact way whether if he was killed he would meet his children in heaven when they too eventually died, and Shaw had struggled to speak to him in terms that could understand. He had been killed hours later.

'The war's over, Guthrie,' insisted Shaw. Guthrie watched him impassively, still holding out the box. Shaw tried to grab the man by his shoulders, but somehow could not reach him. 'Don't you understand, man?' pleaded Shaw. 'The war's over, you don't have to die. *You don't have to die.*'

'It'll never be over, Padre,' said Guthrie, with a sickly grin. 'We're in hell.'

The face of Guthrie had now become the face of King Basil, contorted in his last dying agony. Shaw then felt the lever on the box rising in his hands, impossibly high, forcing his arms in front of his face as if he were elevating the Host.

His uniform was now overlaid with a voluminous surplice, and he felt the words of the Order for Holy Communion pour from his mouth without volition: 'Take, eat, this is my body which is given for you: do this in remembrance of me.'

He then plunged the lever down and the sky exploded in flame. The last thing he saw was a rock hurtling towards his face. He threw up his arms in front of his face, and then woke up, yelling wordlessly.

The bedroom in the vicarage was icily cold; Shaw realised he had kicked the eiderdown off his bed. He picked it up off the floor and covered himself with it as his mind groped back into consciousness. There was no sound except the ticking of the alarm clock on table between his and his wife's bed.

He prayed briefly under his breath, the collect from Evening Prayer.

'Lighten our darkness, we beseech thee, O Lord; and by thy great mercy defend us from all perils and dangers of this night; for the love of thy only Son, our Saviour, Jesus Christ. *Amen.'*

'Amen,' whispered Mrs Shaw from her bed. Shaw lit the small electric lamp on the bedside table and turned to his wife. 'I'm sorry, I must have woken you.'

'No, it's alright,' said his wife. 'I couldn't sleep anyway. You must have been having an awfully bad dream.'

'I was. But it's over now.'

'You called something out but I couldn't make out what it was. Was it about the war again?'

'Yes. A theme which has an annoying habit of recurring. I did not fight in the war and received no injuries; for my unconscious mind to dwell on it seems an indulgence.'

'I did think about waking you but one hears stories about that causing harm.'

'I think that is somnambulists.' Shaw thought for a moment. 'I wonder if there was, perhaps, a meaning in it.'

'In your dream? A sort of premonition?'

'No. I don't mean in a superstitious way. I believe my mind may be trying to make sense of something I did not realise at the time.'

'Oh Lucian dear, you're overwrought. We've both had a terrible shock.'

'Indeed. You more than I. I am sorry that you and Peggy had to be involved.'

'Oh don't worry about Peggy,' said Mrs Shaw brightly. 'She rather relished the excitement I think.' She paused and reached out to grasp her husband's hand. 'You don't think those men will come back, do you?'

'Superintendent Gregory thinks it unlikely,' replied Shaw. 'They have officers searching from them and it would be to no advantage to them to return here. They will wish to get as far away as possible.'

'It's so dreadful not being able to talk to anyone about it,' said Mrs Shaw. 'I'm sure Hettie suspected something when we turned up with that detective.'

'It is a matter of national security,' replied Shaw. 'If the king's death is made public, it could prejudice the investigation. This is no ordinary murder, it is an assassination.'

Mrs Shaw shivered. '"Ordinary murder". It sounds so matter of fact. And I shall have to go around doing my parish duties pretending as if nothing had happened.'

'As will I, my dear,' said Shaw. 'Now, let us try to sleep.'

They kissed and Shaw turned off the light. He fell asleep, dreamlessly this time, as the words of Bridges' hymn echoed and re-echoed in his head until they were lost in a deep chasm of silence.

*

The following morning, Gregory and Carter sat in the interview room in the main police station in Ipswich. The local force were allowing Special Branch to use it, under terms of strict secrecy. Gregory would have preferred to be in his headquarters in London, but the journey was too far to attempt every day and so for the time being he had to put up with borrowed facilities. He lit a De Reske, the first of the day, to take away the taste of the congealed breakfast he had been served in his digs.

Curse the provinces, he thought to himself. He missed his little brand-new modern bachelor flat in London, where meals could be ordered by telephone and brought up the back stairs by one of the staff, and where he could enjoy eating them on his own while listening to the wireless.

Instead, while working on this case, he had to sit in a draughty Victorian parlour, eating cold fried eggs and listening to the bawdy jokes of the commercial travellers staying in the same establishment. Carter, he noticed, who had stayed in the same boarding house, did not seem to mind; Gregory assumed he was simply relieved to no longer have to play the part of a subservient butler.

Gregory sighed and took a deep drag on his cigarette. He turned to Carter, who sat opposite him at a pockmarked metal table.

'Rotten luck about those two spies,' said Gregory. 'Why did that local copper have to kill the blighters?'

Carter shrugged. 'Far as I can tell, he had no choice. They shot first.'

'If he'd only winged them we might have got some information out of them,' replied Gregory.

'We, sir?' asked Carter. 'They're nothing to do with us. Whitehall's made that clear. It was hard enough getting the simple information from Intelligence that the two men were dead.'

'What about the jewels? Are you sure they didn't have them?'

'Not according to the Intelligence fellows. All they know is they're Fenekslavians. Had letters of introduction on them to do with some factory visit, but that was most likely a cover story.'

'Who's on the case?'

'Major Wheatley. Came down on the night train.'

'That oaf. Met him once or twice. One of those types who got commissioned at the end of the war only because there was nobody else left alive.'

Carter laughed, which was unusual for him. 'Never mind sir,' he said. 'At least we can concentrate on the cook now.'

'And the husband,' said Gregory. 'Get anything out of him just now?'

'No sir. Still refuses to talk until he can see his wife.'

'Hmm, we can't hold him for much longer, but he might be a useful bargaining tool. We'll see if Mrs Walters is a bit more co-operative today, shall we?'

'She's certainly our best lead since we got the post-mortem report from the doctor,' said Carter.

'Yes,' replied Gregory. 'Shot with a .30 calibre pistol round, at fairly close range, so we can rule out that hunting rifle being fired from the gun room.'

'Does that mean we can drop Miss Garnham from our enquiries?' said Carter.

'Not just yet, but we'd better focus our efforts on Ana Walters for now. I had a trunk call from the Home Office just now and they want this cleared up sharpish.'

Ana had been arrested last night, after Zorard confirmed it was the house's cutlery in her bag, but she was yet to be charged with murder; Gregory knew he had to act fast before word got out and the whole country went into a Red scare, like the one he recalled had happened in America a few years previously.

A few moments later there was a knock at the door, and Ana entered, escorted by a grim-looking woman police constable. Despite a night in the cells of a police station, Ana still looked strikingly beautiful, thought Gregory, particularly in contrast to the plain officer next to her. As a confirmed bachelor he had given up dwelling on such thoughts long ago, but they still surfaced from time to time. He blinked and stubbed out his cigarette on the ashtray on the table.

'Sit down please, Walters,' said Gregory.

Ana remained standing and stared at Gregory.

'Where is my child?' she demanded.

'Sit down please. Your daughter is perfectly well. We have a welfare officer and a woman police constable checking on her and your father-in-law.'

'I don't believe you.'

'You've got no choice. Now sit down.'

Ana sat, facing Gregory and Carter opposite her at the

table, but she stared resolutely at Gregory. Her eyes and the bone structure of her face momentarily made him think of impossibly ancient things; of horsemen sweeping across the Carpathians into the vast plains of eastern Europe.

Gregory cleared his throat. 'The sooner you co-operate, the sooner you'll be home with your husband and kiddie.'

'Very well,' said Ana. 'But I have told you everything already.'

'I know, but I'm not satisfied yet. Let's go through it again. Where were you when the king was shot?'

'I was in the kitchen, preparing the king's supper.'

'And you heard a gunshot?'

'Yes. From near the room they call the drawing room.'

'What then?'

'I already told you.'

'Tell me again.'

Ana sighed. 'I went to the drawing room and met the others.'

'Did anyone see you in the kitchen?'

'No, I was alone.'

'Did you see Zorard being shot at later?'

'No. And you cannot say it was I who did it. Others were with me in the hall when that happened. The priest also.'

'I know. Just checking. All right then. Let's move forward a bit. Why did you bash my sergeant over the head?'

Ana looked at Carter for the first time. The detective instinctively touched the back of his head, still sore from the assault.

'He had a gun and tried to stop us leaving the house. How did I know he was a policeman?'

'Fair enough,' said Gregory, who noted the look of annoyance on Carter's face. 'Now what happened after you and the other women decided to leave the house?'

'Mrs Burward and that one called Miss Garnham went by the back of the house. I went by the front.'

'Why didn't you stay together?'

'Because I did not want to run away while the Holy Crown and Sword of Saint Fenek were stolen.'

'Why should you care about that?'

'You cannot understand. You are not a Fenekslavian. To us the crown is…is more than life itself.'

'Sounds a bit mystic to me. You're not a Catholic are you? Or that other lot – Orthodox, is it?'

'No. But I still believe there are things we cannot understand in this world. Our country was promised the protection of the Holy Virgin when Saint Fenek was crowned. If the crown is lost, Fenekslavia is lost.'

Carter laughed again. 'You Reds are supposed to hate all that stuff,' he said.

'I am not a communist.'

'Your husband is,' said Gregory.

'No, he is socialist. It is different. Where is he?'

'Helping us with our enquiries, just as you are,' continued the Superintendent. 'All right, so you wanted to stop the jewels being stolen. How could you do that if you were on your own, unarmed?'

'I was going to watch and then follow who took them. But when I passed the front of the house, I saw Zorard put the bag on the front step. He saw me and called out.'

'What did he say?'

'We spoke in Fenekslavian. He told me to get away, that I was at risk, that I could be killed.'

'And what did you say?'

'Nothing. I did not want anybody to know I was there, so I kept quiet, and hid in the bushes.'

'What happened then?

'I heard a man approaching, so I hid myself further in the trees.'

'That must have been Tillotson,' interjected Carter. 'Coming back to his post after having a…'

'Yes, thank you Carter,' said Gregory. He turned back to Ana.

'Then what happened?'

'When I looked back at the door, the bag was gone, and I could not see anybody around.'

'Did you see any footprints in the snow?'

Ana frowned. 'I can't remember. There were some, but I think they were my own, from when I walked around the house. I could not see any others but it is possible there were some.'

'What did you do then?'

'I heard a whistle and then your men captured me.'

'And after that Mr Zorard claimed you stole the jewels. Now, why would he say that?'

'I don't know,' said Ana. 'I think he hates and suspects me because I am, in his country, a lower-class person. A peasant.'

'Come now, he must have had more of a reason than that to suspect you of being a thief.'

'You do not understand our people. When two Fenekslavians meet abroad, there is always a disagreement.'

Ana sat silently, staring ahead of her.

Carter broke the silence. 'Mr Zorard told us last night he'd had his suspicions about you for a while, and wasn't surprised when we later told him some of the silver was found in your bag. If truth be told I thought you were a shifty parcel of goods myself while I was working undercover.'

'Taking a few forks and spoons is one thing,' said

Gregory, 'but carrying a gun in your handbag – well, that's a much more serious matter.'

'I told you last night, I have never seen that gun before,' insisted Ana.

'So you say,' continued Gregory. 'But we've found out something this morning from the post-mortem we didn't know last night. The king was killed by a bullet of the same type used in that pistol. We've ordered a ballistics report and I'm pretty certain we'll prove a match.'

Ana gasped. For the first time she appeared to lose her composure.

Gregory pressed in for the kill. 'There are no fingerprints on that pistol – we've checked – but everything else points to the fact that you killed the king and stole the jewels.'

'No!' hissed Ana. 'I didn't…you cannot prove…'

'Look,' urged Gregory. 'You're a foreigner – all right, you've married an Englishman, but that won't count for much with a jury because he's a Red with a criminal record, like your father-in-law. You're from Fenekslavia, meaning you could have written that note that got thrown through the window. You've been found with stolen goods and a pistol, a pistol that just happens to have been used to assassinate a former king. Nobody can account for your movements when it happened, and your husband won't speak a word in your defence.'

Tears began to appear in Ana's eyes. 'You spoke to my husband?'

Gregory felt a twinge of pity for the girl, but brushed it aside as he felt his quarry finally being run to ground.

'Yes. And he's refusing to speak up for you.'

Ana sniffed. 'All right. I admit it, that I took the silver things. That was my only plan, the only reason I went to work there. To take small things from the king, and to sell them and send the money to help the people in Fenekslavia who he abandoned. It would be a kind of justice. But to take a gun and kill him? It would be insane. Why would I do it?'

'That's just what we asked ourselves, Walters,' said Gregory. 'But late last night one of our men finally managed to get some information over the radio-telephone from the British Embassy in Kecsprem.'

Ana's eyes widened. 'The British Embassy?'

'Yes,' replied Gregory. 'A bit of a long shot and a devil of a telephone bill for us to pay, but it was worth it. The Reds, it seems, are no longer worried about the records of the old regime in Fenekslavia being seen – in fact they're encouraging people to see them as they think it discredits capitalism, or some such. Well our man in Kecsprem found the secret police had a rather interesting file. It was fortunate you told us your maiden name yesterday. Malicsko. It's rare in your country, apparently.'

Ana swallowed. 'It is about my father.'

'Yes,' said Gregory, quietly. 'Our man's Fenekslavian is a bit rusty, but he got the jist of what was in the file – your father was court-martialled and executed, and a plea for clemency from your mother was personally turned down by the king. Something about making an example to the peasants, as the war was going so badly.

'So you see, Walters, you do have a motive for killing the king. He killed your father, or as good as. And if you stole a few spoons, what would stop you stealing the crown jewels as well? I think that, along with everything else, will be enough to convince a jury. Why don't you just confess?'

Ana looked horrified, and her gaze flicked from one detective to the other. 'It cannot be…' she whispered.

'What did you do with the jewels?' asked Carter.

'I...nothing,' replied Ana. 'I told you, when I looked back at the doorstep they were gone.'

'Come along,' said Carter. 'I don't believe that. I think you either hid them somewhere in the grounds, or, since the search we organised at first light hasn't revealed anything, it's more likely you threw them away for someone else to collect. Tillotson said you were close enough to the hedge to do that before you were caught.'

Ana swallowed rapidly, and was silent.

'It won't have done you any good, anyway,' said Gregory. 'Mr Zorard informed us last night that the jewels taken were replicas.'

'What…? whispered Ana. A look of abject confusion had crossed her face.

'You heard,' said Gregory. 'Fakes. Paste jewels used for public appearances by the king. Worth a couple of quid at most. The real ones are in London. We're arranging to have them moved somewhere safer. So whoever you gave them to, whoever you're working for, is going to be rather disappointed I should think.'

Ana broke down in tears, while the two detectives and the stony-faced woman police constable watched in silence.

Chapter Ten

Shaw's day passed much like any other weekday; he read the daily office of Morning Prayer in church, which had an even lower attendance than normal due to the bitterly cold weather; he did some parish visiting and worked on his sermon for Christmas Day.

He noticed at luncheon that his wife appeared worried, but that she was trying to hide it with a sort of brittle cheerfulness. She jumped slightly when the telephone bell rang in the hallway of the vicarage, shortly after they had finished their meal.

Hettie entered the dining room. 'If you please, sir,' she said to Shaw, 'there's a man on the telephone for you.'

'Did he give a name?' murmured Shaw, as he wiped his mouth with his napkin and stood up from the table.

'No sir,' said the maid. 'Just said it was urgent.'

Shaw went into the hallway and picked up the telephone.

'Shaw speaking,' he said, with slight trepidation.

'Gregory here,' said the voice at the end of the line. 'I didn't give my name as I'd rather your servant didn't get suspicious.'

'Of course,' replied Shaw. He noticed out of the corner of his eye that Hettie was watching from the kitchen door.

'How may I be of assistance?' he asked.

'I'm in your neck of the woods,' said Gregory. 'Just been to clear up a few details at The Larches. I wonder, could we meet somewhere? Somewhere quiet. I've some news for you.'

'We could meet at the church,' said Shaw. 'It's a little cold I'm afraid, but certainly quiet.'

'That's all right,' said Gregory. 'I'm used to hanging around in the freezing cold anyway. I've just had lunch in your local pub – the George, that's where I'm telephoning from – so I'll leave my car there and walk to you.'

Shaw made his excuses to his wife and to Hettie, stating that he was going out on church business, which to an extent was true. A few minutes later, he and Superintendent Gregory sat in a pew at the back of the small nave of All Saints' church, their breath visible in the chilly air of the church as they spoke.

'As I said, Mr Shaw,' said Gregory, turning his hat in his hands, 'I've some news for you. You can tell Mrs Shaw that she needn't worry about those men who attacked her and Mrs Marchant last night. They've been found.'

'That will be a relief,' said Shaw. 'My wife was understandably worried that some sort of reprisal might take place.'

'There won't be any reprisals, sir. Not from those two. They're dead. An armed police constable was obliged to shoot them when they resisted arrest on the London road.'

Shaw sighed. Even though the men had clearly been a threat, he remembered the words of the poet John Donne: 'each man's death diminishes me, for I am involved in mankind.'

'Thank you for letting me know,' said Shaw. 'It will at least put my wife's mind at rest. Will she be required to give evidence?'

'Not at this stage,' said Gregory. 'The whole thing's still completely hush-hush. I've just been speaking to Mrs Marchant however, and she's agreed to identify the bodies of the men. She said she'd rather spare your wife that task.'

'That is good of her,' said Shaw. 'Are you any closer to solving the case? Presumably the two men were the killers?'

Gregory rubbed his chin and momentarily looked around him at the whitewashed interior of the little church.

'We've made an arrest,' he said slowly. 'Ana Walters, the cook. The pistol used to kill the king was found in her handbag and there is some other incriminating evidence as well.'

'Other evidence?' asked Shaw. 'Do you mean she has been found in possession of the imitation crown jewels?'

'Not exactly. But I'm pretty certain she's hidden them somewhere or given them to someone. Her face was a picture when I told her the real ones are in a safe deposit box in London.'

'That is, at least, a small blessing,' said Shaw.

'Yes. Mr Zorard's agreed to my suggestion to have them taken somewhere safer under police escort in the next couple of days. So that's one thing I don't have to worry about. We're expecting to charge Walters shortly and that will, I hope, be that. We've had to let her husband go due to a lack of evidence, but we'll be keeping an eye on him.'

Shaw noticed an uncertain tone in the detective's voice. 'Forgive me, Superintendent,' he said, 'but you sound unsure.'

'I shouldn't be telling you this,' replied Gregory, 'but I feel I can trust you. My sergeant's convinced Walters is guilty, and I've had the Home Office breathing down my neck, or at least, down my telephone, as well,' said Gregory. 'They're unhappy about the idea of foreign assassins wandering the countryside and they want this cleared up.'

'Perhaps they would rather the world thought only that one person was involved, rather than a conspiracy?' ventured Shaw.

'That's exactly what I think they want,' said Gregory. 'And I don't think Walters was working with those agents. But everything does seem to point to her being involved somehow.'

There was a brief pause; Shaw could tell the man wanted to get something off his chest, and in his experience of those who wished to unburden themselves, it was better to remain silent and allow them to do so without prompting.

He did not have to wait long. 'We've had a report from the ballistics boys this morning,' said Gregory. 'We thought at first the king had been shot by a rifle from about twenty yards away.'

'From the gun room, presumably,' said Shaw.

'That's what we thought. The fact that a rifle and spent round were found in there, pointed towards that. But we've now ascertained the shot came from a pistol, from a distance of around eight to sixteen feet, and at a horizontal or very slight downward angle. They don't think it could have come from as far away as the window on the opposite side of the courtyard.'

'But we found a rifle and a spent cartridge when we entered the gun room,' said Shaw. 'We all saw it.'

'Yes, I know,' said Gregory. 'But it's my belief now that that was planted there to throw us off the scent.'

'To make it look, perhaps, as if Miss Garnham was the culprit?'

'I wondered that,' said Gregory. 'But who would do that, and why? Carter told me he put the rifle back in the rack after the shoot, but when you lot found it, it was on the floor with a spent round next to it. The only other person who went in there was Mr Zorard.'

'The only other person that we know of,' corrected Shaw. 'Both Miss Garnham and Mrs Walters could, in theory, have gone in there.'

'True enough,' said Gregory. 'But neither Garnham nor Zorard are particularly strong suspects. I can't see what motive Zorard would have for being involved in any of this – as far as I can see he's a fanatical anti-Red. And Carter reckons Garnham and King Basil were genuinely in love. No, I think it was Walters all right – she had the means, the motive and the opportunity.'

'What motive could she have?' asked Shaw. 'As I understand it, she barely knew the king, having only been in his employment for a few days,' said Shaw.

'Turns out he gave the order for her father to be executed back in the old country,' replied Gregory. 'She must have loathed him.'

Shaw murmured in agreement, then thought for a moment about what Gregory had said about the pistol.

'Something troubles me, Superintendent,' he said. 'Until now I assumed that the king was shot with a rifle from the gun room.'

'Why did you assume that?' asked Gregory. 'He could have been shot from just outside the window, and the ballistics report makes it pretty clear that's what happened.'

'I assumed it because there were no footprints on the snow in the courtyard. If somebody stood outside the window, would there not have been prints?'

'When did you look outside?' said Gregory. 'Before or

after the king was shot?'

Shaw paused and thought for a moment. 'Afterwards. I looked when we discovered Soames…I mean, Carter, trying to get in through the corridor window. I remember looking now. There were no footprints in the snow. So then, how could an assassin have stood outside the window?'

'But if I remember what Carter said rightly, when you and Zorard caught him, that was some time after the king was shot,' said Gregory. 'It was snowing on and off all the time last night and the prints could have been covered. Carter had to walk from the garage to the house when he climbed through the window, and he must have left prints unless he levitated. So any prints in the snow would have been covered up quickly by fresh snowfall. I don't think we can rely on them as evidence, much as I'd like to.

'It's perfectly possible,' continued Gregory, 'for Walters to have gone to the gun room, thrown the stone through the gun room window, gone outside and shot the king through the drawing room window, then gone back to the kitchen, with all her prints covered up later by snowfall. Zorard said he saw someone running away when he looked out of the window after the stone was thrown. So there must have been prints, you just didn't look until they were gone.'

'But why would Mrs Walters go to the trouble of throwing the stone from the gun room?' asked Shaw.

'Hmm, you've got me there, I admit,' said Gregory. 'I wish my sergeant had as keen a brain as you, Mr Shaw.'

Shaw looked steadily at Gregory. 'You are aware, Superintendent, that I was involved in a murder case in this village earlier this year?'

'Yes,' replied Gregory. 'What of it?'

'I ask because the officer investigating the case, an

Inspector Ludd, was not happy, at least initially, about my taking an interest in the case and offering him my theories. Similarly, I do not wish to intrude upon your investigation by prolonging this conversation.'

'I see,' said Gregory. 'It might interest you to know, Mr Shaw, that it's because of that case I feel able to talk to you. I've been able to look at some of the files relating to that case at the station in Ipswich, and Ludd wrote about you in glowing terms in his report.'

Shaw felt his face flush slightly, which he hoped was not visible in the winter gloom of the church.

'I've no objection,' continued Gregory, 'to a little outside perspective once in a while, especially in a case that has got me a bit stumped. I don't mind telling you, Mr Shaw, I've got doubts about this one.'

'Very well, Superintendent,' said Shaw. 'You will, then, perhaps indulge my theorising a little longer. If, as you say, Mrs Walters is the killer, then who fired at Mr Zorard when he attempted to leave the house? It could not have been Mrs Walters, as she was with myself and others at the time, in the hall.'

'I've thought about that,' said Gregory. 'That could have been the Red agents, the ones we think were working with Walters, and that your wife disturbed in the lane. If they weren't both lying on a slab in Ipswich mortuary I might know a bit more.'

'Have you drawn any conclusions from the cartridge case that I found by the back door?'

'I've had a ballistics report on that as well,' said Gregory. 'It's fairly easy to tell if a bullet was fired from a particular gun, due to the pattern of grooving formed by the barrel. It's a slightly harder task to prove a spent cartridge case alone came from a particular gun. But our boys noticed a pattern of small scratches on the casing which fits with a slight flaw in the loading mechanism of that pistol, so we're pretty sure whoever fired at Zorard used the pistol that we found in Walters' handbag.'

'But I have already said, it could not have been Mrs Walters who fired at Mr Zorard,' insisted Shaw. 'She was directly in front of me when it happened.'

'I know that, Mr Shaw. 'It suggests someone else was involved – an accomplice of Walters. '

'One of the foreign agents?'

'Perhaps, or her husband. But he's unlikely because as far as we know, he didn't arrive until the last minute, after all the shooting had taken place.'

'I see,' mused Shaw. 'I take your point that this is a most extraordinary case. One further thing however – if we are to assume that Mrs Walters is the culprit, and fired through the drawing room window rather than from the gun room, why then was the gun room window broken also?'

'I can see why Ludd spoke highly of you,' said Gregory. 'I think you're in the wrong vocation. Matter of fact I thought about this myself. The only explanation I can think of is that Walters broke it at the same time as she laid out the hunting rifle and the spent cartridge on the gun room floor. To make it look as if somebody – perhaps Elsie Garnham – had fired through the window of the gun room. To throw us off the scent, as it were.'

'I know very little about this sort of thing,' said Shaw, 'but would it not have been simpler to have merely left the window open, to give the suggestion that it had been fired through? Breaking a window risked attracting attention.'

'I thought that too,' said Gregory. 'But when we had a look at it, we found the window doesn't open very far up; the sash is broken it seems. It won't open enough to allow someone a decent throw. So she broke it at some point, probably while you lot were having tea.'

'But surely we would have heard…' began Shaw. Just then there was the noise of boots scraping on stone, and Shaw looked up to see Tompkins, the choirmaster, entering the church. He squinted through the gloom at the two men.

'Ah, vicar,' said Tompkins, whose thin frame was heavily bulked out by a tweed coat and college scarf wound several times round his neck. 'Not disturbing anything, am I?'

'Of course not, Mr Tompkins,' said Shaw. 'Forgive me, I forgot the time. Choir practice today, of course.'

'No rest for the wicked, vicar,' said Tompkins cheerfully. 'We're practicing the descants for the carol service today, and some of them are devilishly tricky.'

Shaw wondered what Tompkins would think if he knew the sort of devilish trickery that had just been discussed by him and Gregory, but before he could answer, the Superintendent stood up and walked to the door.

'Well thank you for your time, Mr Shaw,' he said, as the door was opened for him. 'That was most helpful. I'll be in touch again soon if I need any more help with – ' He paused as he glanced at Tompkins, who was setting out music sheets in the choir stalls – 'with this particular aspect of parish business. Good day to you.'

*

Shaw sat for a while at the back of the church, mulling over what Gregory had told him. Tompkins switched on the dim electric lights near the altar, installed by Shaw himself when he became incumbent, to replace the ancient oil lamps that had been there for generations. There had been resistance at first, Shaw recalled, as some parishioners expected the church to be lit up like a cinema foyer, but he had ensured that the effect was subtle. 'Casting a dim religious light,' as the poet John Milton had put it.

The choristers began to shuffle into the church from the vestry door; a few retired farm hands and a gaggle of boys attracted by the sixpence per service pocket money that they could earn, rather than by any great love for the Anglican choral tradition. The numbers of boys always increased after Advent in line with the increase in special services; the boys then usually fell away after Trinity Sunday in summer, when there was a paucity of festivals and better paid work for them on the local farms.

Shaw watched from the back of the church, unseen, as the choir began to rehearse Christmas carols, conducted by Tompkins, who had now removed his overcoat to allow his arms to move more freely. Shaw allowed his thoughts to drift away, carried by the ancient songs that had been sung in that place for generations. A young boy sang, awkwardly at first, but then with confidence, the descant for *Good King Wenceslas*:

Mark my footsteps, good my page
Tread thou in them boldly
Thou shalt find the winter's rage
Freeze thy blood less coldly.

Was King Wenceslas a Fenekslavian? thought Shaw. He decided that he probably was not, but certainly came from somewhere around that part of Europe in a similar country, such as Bohemia or Moravia. The carol seemed to stir something in the depths of his brain. The descant ended and the choir joined in unison for the final verse, as the organist swelled the sound of the organ to its loudest level by pulling out various stops on the console.

In his master's steps he trod,
where the snow lay dinted...

Shaw awoke from his reverie, conscious that he was late for afternoon tea. He chided himself for selfish mental reflection when he ought to be putting his wife's mind at rest about the possibility of the two foreign agents seeking her out for reprisals. He stood up and left the church unseen, then hurried to the vicarage as the sounds of the ancient carol faded away behind him.

*

A few hours later, and over a thousand miles away, a frozen dawn was breaking over Kecsprem, the capital of Fenekslavia. Unlike in England, here there were few preparations being made for Christmas, at least in public. The churches, although not completely closed, were strongly discouraged by the new regime from holding services.

A few black-clad elderly women crept by the side door into the city's ancient, crumbling cathedral for a whispered mass, and to light candles and say prayers at the shrines of the Holy Virgin and Saint Fenek, king and martyr; prayers were also said, in low tones, for King Basil the Second, that he might one day be returned from exile. These pious individuals, of course, could not know that King Basil had been exiled to a place from which there would be no return until the Last Day.

In his apartment overlooking the icy, black Tulavista

river, the unshaven man was woken by the insistent sound of the telephone bell. He immediately roused himself and brushed himself down; he had slept in his clothes, too tired to remove them after falling asleep only a few hours before.

He picked up the receiver and immediately recognised the voice of a fellow army officer, who spoke on a crackling, whistling line, typical of the poorly maintained Kecsprem telephone system.

'There has been news from London,' said the officer. 'Agent C...'

'Not on the telephone,' barked the unshaven man, shouting to make himself heard over the sound of a tram which rattled and screeched on the boulevard outside. 'Meet me in Karl Marx Square in ten minutes.'

'Where?' asked the man, in a puzzled voice.

The unshaven man sighed. 'The place which was called King Basil Square. You were on the committee that approved the change of name, at least try to remember it.'

He put down the receiver and shrugged on his military greatcoat and peaked cap with its hastily sewn on red star in place of a regimental badge. Strictly speaking he should have strapped on his cutlass also, but the old royal uniform codes were being routinely ignored now, and the thing was so heavy anyway.

A few minutes later he was strolling with the officer, a lieutenant in the intelligence corps, in the once well-maintained gardens of King Basil Square, which had now fallen into wintry disarray.

'As I mentioned earlier,' said the young lieutenant, 'we have made contact with Agent C. She managed to get a coded message to us via the Russian Embassy in London. I am afraid, sir...' The man hesitated.

'Afraid of what?' demanded the unshaven man.

'Afraid that it is bad news,' said the lieutenant, swallowing hard.

'I shall judge that. Tell me what you have heard.'

'Very well, sir. Agent C made contact with agents A and B briefly after the plan was put into action.'

'The plan was successful?'

The lieutenant swallowed again and paused. 'No sir. It failed. They did not manage to penetrate the grounds of the house. Two women interrupted them.'

'Two women?' growled the unshaven man. 'Why did the imbeciles not deal with them?'

'They…attempted to sir, but the women fought them.'

The unshaven man stopped walking and gaped. 'They were scared away, by two English women?'

'There was also a dog, a large, vicious one. Agent A was badly bitten.'

'Tell these idiots to try again.'

'Unfortunately sir….they cannot.'

'Why on earth not? What are we paying them for?'

'We cannot be sure sir…the English have not reported this in the press, but…from what Agent C was able to find out, the other two are dead. Shot by the English police.'

The unshaven man was too angry to speak for a moment. He struggled to remain calm.

'How is that possible? The English police are not armed. Everybody knows that.'

'It seems they are armed on certain occasions, sir,' said the young lieutenant, apologetically. 'We did not plan for that.'

The unshaven man slumped down on a bench, still coated with frost and icicles, and gazed at the blood-red sun beginning to appear beyond the distant cathedral.

'Tell Agent C that she must put the back-up plan into operation.'

'But it will be too dangerous, sir,' protested the lieutenant. 'Agent C thinks the secret police are watching her. The authorities will be suspicious, the king will have gone into hiding. The turncoat Zorard will be protecting him…'

'I don't care,' barked the unshaven man. 'And don't mention that man's name again. He is dead to us. If Agent C cannot kill the king, she must at least bring the jewels to us. That is an order.'

The lieutenant, who had not sat down on the bench, clicked his heels to attention, and began to make the old royalist salute, then corrected himself and performed it in the new Russian style. He turned and walked briskly away.

Only a few days, thought the unshaven man, as he watched the young lieutenant weave his way through the early morning traffic on Lenin Avenue. Only a few days before I have to make my report to the Russians. And if C fails, I fail. Nothing less than the death of the king and the return of the full complement of crown jewels will satisfy them.

He pictured his epaulettes pulled off and cutlass ceremonially broken, then being left alone with a glass of *poplinka* and a revolver, the traditional self-imposed death penalty for unforgivable failure.

He pushed the image out of his mind. The Russians would have no time for such romantic nonsense, he decided. A firing squad would be the best he could hope for. With a shiver, he stood up and began walking back to his apartment.

*

That day, Shaw did not have a great deal to do, at least in the morning, as his curate, Laithwaite, was taking Morning Prayer. At breakfast he was pleased to see that his wife seemed in better spirits. They could not talk openly due to the presence of Hettie, but from their private conversations in the bedroom he ascertained she was relieved that no foreign assassins were going to come after her, and that the police were close to charging the principal suspect.

The modicum of peace was interrupted by the ringing of the telephone bell in the little hallway of the vicarage. Shaw assumed it must be some matter of parish business about which he had forgotten – or perhaps a parishioner in need of help. He was surprised, however, when Hettie told him who it was on the line.

'Please sir, it's a Miss Garnham,' said the maid. 'She says it's urgent.'

'Thank you Hettie,' said Shaw, putting down his cup of half-drunk English Breakfast tea and exchanging curious glances with Mrs Shaw.

Elsie's voice sounded worried. 'I must speak with you, vicar,' she said insistently. 'I didn't know who else to call. Something's…happened.'

'Very well,' said Shaw calmly. 'What has happened?'

'Not on the telephone,' said Elsie. 'Can you come round to my cottage, as soon as possible?'

Within a few moments Shaw had mounted his bicycle, and was negotiating the ice and slush on the lane which led to The Larches. Twenty minutes later he had arrived at the small cottage, a few hundred yards from the main house, in which the late King Basil had installed his bride-never-to-be.

In any other circumstances he would have admired the prettiness of the little building, constructed presumably for some sort of gardener or game-keeper.

It was a scaled-down version of its larger neighbour, complete with imitation tudor beams and leaded windows. Shaw, however, sensed something was wrong and concentrated on the matter in hand as Elsie showed him into the little parlour.

He looked around to see the place in disarray. Doors and drawers had been flung open and items strewn about.

'It happened last night,' said Elsie. She had a look of fear mixed with steely resolve about her. 'I walked into the village to go to the George. I don't normally drink in pubs on my own – well, a lady can get a reputation, can't she? – but I just wanted to be with other people. When I came back I found the lock had been picked somehow and the place had been ransacked – my bedroom as well. I shouldn't have gone but I just wanted to get out for a bit. I used to like this cottage but since…the other night…'

'Of course, of course,' said Shaw, looking around him at the confusion. 'You have sent for the police, I assume? Superintendent Gregory's men are I believe, still on the premises at The Larches.'

'They've all gone now,' said Elsie. 'I can't tell them about this anyway. That's why I called you.'

'But Miss Garnham,' protested Shaw, 'this is clearly a burglary. It is your duty to inform the authorities.'

'I know,' said Elsie. She slumped into a chintz-covered armchair and looked steadily at Shaw. 'Sit down, vicar, and I'll tell you why I can't.'

Shaw crossed to the sofa and moved a book aside before sitting down. Its title was *Teach Yourself Fenekslavian*.

Elsie noticed Shaw looking at the book. She picked it up and put it with some other books that had been hurled off the bookcase.

'I was teaching myself the language, for when I became queen,' she said. 'I got quite good at it, surprisingly. Silly really, there's no point now of course.

'Anyway,' she continued, 'before he...died...Basil gave me something. The Ring of Fidelity. Part of the crown jewels of Fenekslavia. They consist of the crown of Saint Fenek, the Sword of Justice and the Ring of Fidelity. A few other bits and bobs, maces and so on, but those were the three most important things, Basil said, that were needed for royal events. The ring was worn by the queens of Fenekslavia going back donkey's years.'

'Do you mind if I smoke my pipe?' asked Shaw. 'I find it helps me to concentrate.'

'Be my guest,' said Elsie. 'I'd offer you tea but there's nothing here. My meals are brought over by Mrs Burward.'

'That is quite alright,' said Shaw. He filled his pipe with Three Nuns, lit it, and sat back in the armchair. 'Go on, please,' he said.

'Well, Basil let me have the ring. Sort of on loan, but it didn't matter because I was going to be entitled to wear it as soon as we were married. But he said, don't show it to anyone and don't tell anyone you've got it. It went against some sort of royal rules, apparently, and he said that lackey of his, Zorard, would have a fit if he knew.'

Elsie poked the little fire in the grate to coax more warmth into the room, then sat back in her chair.

'I don't understand why this means you cannot tell the police that somebody has broken into your cottage,' said Shaw.

'Maybe this will help,' said Elsie. She took a crumpled piece of paper from her pocket and gave it to Shaw. 'Whoever broke in left that on the mat.'

Shaw looked at the paper and saw, hand-written in large capital letters, the following words:

WE KNOW YOU HAVE IT.
LEAVE IT IN A PACKAGE ON THE DOORSTEP.
WE WILL COLLECT AT NOON.
DO NOT ATTEMPT TO STOP US.
IF YOU TELL THE POLICE WE WILL KILL YOU.

Chapter Eleven

Shaw puffed on his pipe, and returned the note to Elsie. 'Miss Garnham,' he said sternly, 'whoever wrote this must be involved with the murder of King Basil. We must telephone Superintendent Gregory immediately. There is not much time. This is the perfect opportunity for his men to make an arrest.'

'I tell you we can't tell the police,' insisted Elsie. 'There's something else.'

Shaw smoked and watched as Elsie took something carefully from her cardigan pocket. She held it out to him. It was a spent cartridge case. 'I found this on the floor of the drawing room, when I went in to see Basil's body. It was under the tea table. I didn't tell the police about it.'

Shaw took the case and examined it. 'A similar type to the one I found by the back door,' he said. 'But why did you not tell the police about it?'

'I…I don't know. At first I thought I'd better take it, in case it got lost or somebody else found it – somebody in the house who didn't want it to be found. Then when the police started asking me questions, I realised I was a suspect.'

'Surely not,' said Shaw, in surprise.

'You didn't hear the way they talked. Especially that

Soames, or Carter or whatever he calls himself. That rifle that was found in the gun room, well they think I used that to shoot Basil with. They didn't say it in so many words, but…'

Shaw leant forward to tap out his pipe on the metal grate of the fire; a little shower of sparks flew out. He blew through the empty pipe to clean it, and sat back in his chair.

'It may interest you to know, Miss Garnham,' he said, 'that the Superintendent informed me yesterday that they have proof that the king was killed not by a rifle, but by a pistol, fired most probably by somebody standing outside the drawing room window.'

Shaw expected this piece of information to improve Elsie's spirits, but it seemed to have the opposite effect.

'Miss Garnham, are you alright?'

'Not really vicar. I've just realised something. Do you know much about guns?'

'Not a great deal, other than what I picked up in my army chaplaincy days.'

'Well I've been around guns all my life. When you fire a pistol – an automatic pistol, that is – the spent casing gets ejected out of the side. It can fly a couple of feet, but that's about all. I found that casing under the tea table. That's about eight feet from the window, I'd say. It couldn't possibly have popped out that far. That means whoever shot Basil did it in that room.'

Shaw met Elsie's hostile gaze with a steady stare. 'That means that the shot was fired either by Mrs Burward, Mr Zorard…or myself.'

'Exactly, vicar. Which means I've got a one in three chance of sitting opposite a murderer at this moment.'

'You surely do not think that I am involved?'

'You tell me. Don't pretend that you don't have any

suspicions about me, either.'

Shaw coughed awkwardly. 'Well, if we are going to cast stones,' he said, referring of course to the famous passage of St John's gospel, 'it is possible, is it not, that the pistol was fired by someone – perhaps even you – from outside the window, and the spent cartridge was retrieved and tossed through immediately afterwards, to give the impression that the weapon had been fired from within the room.'

'Go on,' said Elsie.

'Indeed,' continued Shaw, 'since you did not mention your discovery of the cartridge at the time, you did not even have to throw it through the window. You simply could have kept it on your person, to be used later to incriminate someone.'

'Then why didn't I mention it at the time when I found it?'

Shaw sighed. 'Miss Garnham, this is getting us nowhere. It is fruitless to throw around mutual allegations when the police have an opportunity to make an arrest.'

'You're right of course, vicar,' said Elsie. 'We're over-thinking it. My mind's been in a whirl these last couple of days, and it doesn't help not being allowed to talk to anyone about it. Zorard's polite enough but I can tell he wants me gone as soon as possible. There's Mrs Burward of course – she brings my meals still – but I can tell she doesn't like me much. And the police will say I'm a gold-digger.'

'A gold digger?' asked Shaw, who was unfamiliar with the expression. 'Forgive me, I don't quite follow.'

'A woman on the make,' said Elsie. 'A washed up floozy who got her claws into a rich man and started helping herself to his jewels, then shot him in a fit of anger because he wouldn't make her his queen. That's how they'll frame it. Believe me, I've had dealings with the police before.' She shuddered and folded her arms.

'I do not believe that is their main line of enquiry,' said Shaw. 'In fact, Superintendent Gregory confided to me that his main suspect is Ana Walters.'

'Really?' asked Elsie. 'I always thought it was a bit odd, her turning up out of the blue like that. What's he got on her?'

'Suffice to say there is a certain amount of evidence that she was working in conjunction with Fenekslavian agents.'

'Well I'll be blowed,' said Elsie with a sharp exhalation of breath. 'And here's me thinking they were setting me up for the fall. I still could get pinched for taking that ring, though. I've no proof Basil gave it to me. Well there's no way I'm handing that over to some dirty blackmailers. That was a gift from Basil and I'm keeping it. I'd rather die than give it up.'

'That reminds me,' said Shaw. 'Any value the ring has is sentimental. It is a fake, worth a few shillings at most.'

Elsie gaped. 'What on earth do you mean?'

'Mr Zorard told me. The jewels are replicas for ceremonial occasions. The real ones were placed in a safety deposit box in London after the king's arrival in England. The police are shortly moving them to even greater safety, to prevent any further attempts at theft.'

'But…' protested Elsie. Shaw cut her off with a wave of his hand.

'If I may finish what I was saying, Miss Garnham. The note you received must have been written by whoever took the bag of jewels from the front step of The Larches. They must have realised that the ring was missing, but cannot be aware that the items are replicas. Why would they demand a worthless fake? Therefore if you hand the item over, there will be no financial risk to anyone, and it will enable the police to catch the killers of the late king.'

Shaw watched with a slight sense of alarm as Elsie unbuttoned the top two fastenings of her blouse. 'Are you telling me, vicar,' she said slowly, 'that this is a fake?' She pulled out a fine chain which hung around her neck. Fastened to it was an enormous ring of burnished gold, with a huge diamond set in the top.

Elsie held the ring up in front of her and switched on a little reading lamp on the table next to her. In the beams of the lamp, the jewel sparkled and glistened in a way that no glass ever could.

Shaw leaned forward to examine the stone more closely. He realised he was leaning rather too close to Elsie.

'Here, take it,' she said, removing the chain and passing it to Shaw. He held the ring up to the light and looked within the stone. There was none of the distortion or rainbow colouring that one would see in cheap costume jewellery; instead, the diamond flickered with a clear, brilliant light.

'Where was this kept when the king gave it to you?' asked Shaw, gazing at the ring as he turned it.

'Basil kept the jewels in a cupboard in his office in an ordinary looking bag. He said they managed to smuggle them out from the Royal Palace just before the Reds stormed in.'

'A canvas bag, in a large, mahogany cabinet?'

'That's right,' said Elsie. 'How did you know?'

Shaw looked out of the little leaded windows of the cottage onto the pristine whiteness of the snow-covered lawn outside. The words and music of two hymns intertwined in his imagination, repeating themselves several times in a strange, composite tune.

Sword and crown betray his trust…
Where the snow lay dinted…

Suddenly Shaw felt the pieces of a mental jigsaw fall into place in his brain.

'Do you have a motor car, Miss Garnham?,' he asked.

'Why, yes,' replied Elsie. 'Basil bought a little baby Austin for me. Why do you ask?'

Shaw looked at his watch. 'I need to go to the shops.'

*

'A remarkable piece,' said old Mr Palfrey, squinting at the ring through his jeweller's eyepiece. Shaw watched as the elderly, bent man examined the item carefully. There was no jeweller in Lower Addenham, but Shaw knew that there was one in the nearby market town of Great Netley, as he had recently been there to have his wife's wedding ring reset. Driven by Elsie, Shaw had been able to get there quickly.

He looked out of the dark, stuffy little shop to the street outside, where Elsie sat in the Austin, nervously tapping her gloved fingers on the steering wheel, her breath drifting in clouds around her chic cloche hat.

'A very, very remarkable piece,' said Mr Palfrey. He took out his eyepiece and held the ring to the light. 'A flawless diamond. From eastern Europe I should say, by the setting, or perhaps Russian, and old – very old – possibly even medieval.' He looked at Shaw with a rheumy gaze. 'If you don't mind me asking sir,' he enquired cautiously, 'where did you get this?'

Shaw hesitated before answering, realising he did not need to tell an outright lie. 'It belonged to a recently deceased parishioner from abroad,' he said. 'His...heiress...wishes to have it valued, and asked me, presumably as a trustworthy person, to undertake the task.'

'I see...' said Mr Palfrey. 'Well this heiress is very lucky. I am no expert, and really, this ought to be checked by a specialist, but at a conservative estimate I would value such a ring at at least fifty thousand guineas.'

*

In the police station in Ipswich, Gregory slammed down the telephone at his borrowed desk, drawing curious glances from the local detectives working in the same room. Gregory's other Special Branch detectives had now been sent back to London, and he had been looking forward to leaving himself with Carter once they had charged Ana Walters. The telephone call, however, had put paid to all that.

'There you are, Carter,' said Gregory, as the sergeant wandered into the room holding a green tea-cup and saucer. 'Outside, now.'

Carter had just enough time to place his tea-cup down on the desk of a local detective constable before Gregory dragged him out by his elbow into the corridor. Making sure they could not be overheard, he spoke to Carter in a low tone.

'I've just had our friend Wheatley of military intelligence on the line,' he said. 'Turns out the Fenekslavians had a third operative in the country.'

'Good God,' exhaled Carter. 'Why didn't they tell us earlier?'

'They couldn't be sure. But they've lifted her now.'

'Her?'

'Yes. Working as a domestic servant right here in Suffolk, if you please. One of the men that was shot dead had her address on him.'

'Sloppy beggar,' replied Carter with a sneer. 'Who trained that lot – Fred Karno's?'

'I'll remind you, Detective Sergeant Carter,' said Gregory, 'that you were a sloppy beggar as well – you blew your cover and got bashed on the head by a murder suspect.'

'Sorry, sir,' said Carter, duly admonished. 'Did they get anything out of her?'

'A lot. She's claiming political asylum in England, says she was forced into the espionage game by the Reds in Fenekslavia. They ordered her and the other two to kill King Basil and steal the jewels.'

'Well that's it then sir. Case closed.'

'Not so fast. She says she's never heard of Ana Walters and she wasn't anywhere near The Larches when the king was killed. Wheatley's talked to the householder she worked for, she was on duty all afternoon and evening, serving tea and dinner to half a dozen witnesses.'

'Then the other two agents must have done it.'

'They can't have, according to Wheatley anyway. Those two called by this woman's house and told her the whole plan to kill the king and nab the jewels was off because somebody – presumably Mesdames Shaw and Marchant – interrupted them before they'd even managed to get into the grounds.'

Carter thought for a moment. 'That fits – if memory serves, the women said they fought off the two Fenekslavians a good half hour after the witnesses said the king was shot. But if they didn't do it then who did?'

Gregory angrily tapped a De Reszke on his cigarette

case, clamped his lips down on it and lit it, inhaling deeply.

He sounded calmer after breathing out a long plume of blue smoke. 'I think we've been looking at this all wrong. Thinking it was all about foreign agents creeping about the place. It looks as if none of them was involved.'

'Who did it then, sir? asked Carter, in a confused voice.

'If it was Ana Walters, then what did she do with the jewels?,' replied Gregory. 'We haven't found them in the grounds anywhere, and she can't have thrown them to anyone, at least we don't think so. Her husband was sitting in a police van at that point. That gun in her handbag bothers me as well.'

'Why's that sir?' asked Carter. 'Surely that's a smoking gun. Literally.'

'Yes, but it's too obvious, now that I think about it. Why would she go to all the trouble of killing someone then leave the bally murder weapon in her handbag? She had ample time to dispose of it somewhere we'd never find it.'

Gregory stopped speaking as a tea-lady approached, rattling her wooden trolley along the hard linoleum floor. After she had passed to a safe distance, he resumed speaking.

'Up until now we've assumed old Basil was shot from outside, but what if he wasn't? What if he was shot from *inside* the room?'

'But somebody would have seen someone else come into the room,' said Carter. 'The parson, for example.'

'The parson and everyone else said it was pitch black in that room when the lights went out.'

'Could someone else have got in through the door and done it?'

'Unlikely. Mrs Burward said she was standing right by the door and she would have noticed, surely.'

'But if someone fired from inside the room, the others would have heard the difference in sound, or seen the difference in the muzzle flash.'

'Not necessarily. Would you know the difference in the report or muzzle flash of a pistol going off three feet away as opposed to six?'

'Hmm, I suppose not,' pondered Carter. 'Then what you're saying, sir, is that the king could have been shot by someone in that room. But why? None of them has any motive.'

'Any motive that we know of,' corrected Gregory. 'Maybe we've been looking in the wrong place. Maybe I've let an upper-crust accent and a clerical collar lead me up the garden path and I've let on too much of what I know.'

'Sir?' asked Carter with a puzzled expression.

'Never mind,' said Gregory. 'We're assuming this is all the work of a bunch of foreign agents working with Ana Walters. But what if it's someone working alone?'

'But there has to be another party involved other than the people who were in the drawing room,' insisted Carter. 'If one of those three – Burward, Zorard, or Shaw – is acting alone, then who threw the rock through the window?'

'I don't know,' said Gregory, grinding his cigarette out under his foot on the linoleum, 'but get your hat and coat and bring that car round quick smart. We're going to have to let Walters go soon unless we charge her – but first, we're going to pay another visit to our friends down at The Larches.'

'I see,' said Shaw, 'thank you for trying. Good day to you.' He replaced the telephone receiver onto its cradle, placed a shilling beside it to pay for the call, and walked back into Elsie's sitting room.

'After some considerable effort I was able to speak to a police officer who knew who Superintendent Gregory was,' said Shaw. 'It seems he is working in Ipswich on secondment from London and the telephone number he gave me is only temporary.'

'Is he on his way?' asked Elsie anxiously.

'Unfortunately they were not able to find him. The officer I spoke to thought that he and Sergeant Carter left in their motor car a short while ago. Destination unknown. I have left a message that he is to come here as soon as he is able.'

'It's nearly noon now,' said Elsie, looking at the little long-case clock in the corner of the sitting room. 'I know I didn't want to before, but oughtn't we to telephone the local police?'

Shaw thought for a moment before replying. 'No. We have been charged to keep this matter entirely secret – that is what Superintendent Gregory said – as it concerns matters of national security. To involve the village police at this stage could be disastrous, particularly as they are not armed.'

'Well what on earth do we do?' said Elsie. 'We can't just sit here and let them walk off with a priceless jewel.'

'I do not intend to allow them to,' said Shaw firmly.

'You read the note – they said they'll kill us if we try to stop them.'

'The note referred to *you*, Miss Garnham. Not to me. Whoever is going to collect the jewel will not be expecting me to be in the vicinity. There is unlikely to be suspicion if the local vicar is making a call.'

'I can't risk it,' said Elsie. 'What if the killers…?'

'I am reasonably confident that the killer, or killers, will not personally collect the jewel from your doorstep. It would be too great a risk that their identity could be revealed.'

'I don't understand.'

'There is no time to explain. Miss Garnham, please retain the ring on your person. I will require something of a similar size and weight.'

He looked around the ransacked room and saw a little brass sealing wax stamp lying on a pile of notepaper that had been thrown out of the bureau by the fireplace. He wrapped it in a piece of newspaper and placed it into an envelope, which he handed to Elsie.

'Kindly place this on the front step. Then come back inside and lock the door and do not answer it to anyone until I return or unless Superintendent Gregory gets here. I will leave by the back door.'

Elsie stood up and took the package. 'But what are you…?'

'Please do as I say, Miss Garnham,' said Shaw. He watched as she moved to the front door, and while she was doing so, he slipped out of the back door and mounted his bicycle, then rode a short way down the drive which led to the main road, dismounted and concealed both his person and his bicycle in the hedge.

From this vantage point he could see both the front and the back of the little cottage a hundred yards or so away from him. He would have a clear view of anybody approaching it. In the still, cold air he even fancied he could hear the bell of his own church in the distance chiming twelve. Then there was silence; he wondered for a moment whether he had been seen.

Suddenly he heard the crunching sound of heavy boots on compacted snow; he peered through the dark foliage of the hedge to see a figure trudge past him just a few feet away. Shaw retreated to the furthest recesses of the hedge, so that he would not be seen. After a few seconds he looked out again, and saw the figure, a man dressed in a shabby tweed coat and cap, bending down to pick the package up from the cottage doorstep. He looked around furtively before slipping the package into his coat pocket and in that moment Shaw realised who it was – Griggs, the tramp.

Shaw continued to watch from his hiding place as Griggs trudged back along the drive towards the lane, and as the man passed by he caught a whiff of some foul-smelling tobacco smouldering in a greasy looking pipe; probably the remains of old cigarette stubs picked up off the ground.

Once Griggs had turned onto the lane, Shaw emerged from the hedge and cycled in the same direction. Once at the junction he peered cautiously around the hedge to make sure that Griggs was on the road, and had not seen him. The tramp was walking along the lane back to Lower Addenham, seemingly oblivious to the world around him.

Shaw increased his speed, skidding a little on the slushy lane, and within a few seconds had caught up with Griggs. The man looked around in alarm at the sound of Shaw's bicycle bell.

'Mr Griggs, good day to you,' said Shaw, touching the brim of his hat as he struggled slightly to control his handlebars. 'A fine day for a walk. Perhaps you are out looking for work?'

Griggs looked annoyed but then affected and air of nonchalance. 'Not today thanks vicar. I ain't got time.' He stared straight ahead and continued walking.

'A pity,' replied Shaw. 'As I have a little job for you, that will take up no time at all, and will be considerably to your financial advantage.'

At the word 'financial', a look of low cunning crossed the vagrant's face. He stopped walking, and Shaw slithered his bicycle to a halt and dismounted.

'Oh yus?' asked Griggs. 'What sort of financial are we talking about?'

'That depends, Mr Griggs,' said Shaw. 'Am I correct in saying you have been paid to deliver a package for someone?'

'Oo told yer?' asked Griggs, his eyes narrowing with suspicion.

'I saw you collect it myself, from the cottage up the lane.'

Griggs scowled. 'Been spying on me, has yer?'

Shaw smiled. 'I noticed you while on a…parish visit. May I ask who employed you on the errand?'

Griggs drew himself up. 'No you may not ask, vicar, as the party in question wishes to remain synonymous. And besides, I don't know who he is.'

'But he paid you?'

'Yus, handsomely. Not that it's any business of yourn.'

'Ah but you see, Mr Griggs, it is very much my business. I will be willing to pay double what he is paying you.'

'The gentleman said as I wasn't to give up the parcel to no-one, else I wouldn't get the rest of me money.'

'That is quite all right, Mr Griggs. I do not want the parcel. I merely want to know who paid you and where it is to be delivered.'

'And you'll pay double?'

'Certainly.'

Griggs paused. Shaw suspected that the man was

slowly calculating by what factor he could reasonably inflate his payment before Shaw became suspicious.

'All right vicar,' he finally answered. 'The gent give me a pound afore and promised me another ten bob…I mean, another pound, that is, after I delivered it.'

Shaw smiled, inwardly relieved that Griggs did not realise quite how valuable the information he held could be.

'Very well,' said Shaw. He took out his wallet and extracted his only five pound note, which he carefully unfolded in front of Griggs. The tramp's eyes bulged as he saw the bank note, and Shaw fancied the man was beginning to drool.

Griggs snatched it with grubby fingers and shoved it somewhere deep inside the various layers of cardigans and waistcoats he wore under his overcoat. He looked cautiously around and beckoned Shaw closer toward him.

'Alright vicar. I said I don't know the party's name, and that's the God's honest truth, s'elp me.'

'Very well,' said Shaw. He had not expected the man to have introduced himself. 'Could you describe him?'

'Not much to describe,' sniffed Griggs. 'Well dressed sort. Nice clothes, expensive, like yer sees in Burton's window, none of yer rubbish. Couldn't see his face as he had a big muffler wrapped all round it and his hat pulled down over his eyes.'

'When did he approach you?'

'Not long after nine this forenoon. I knowed it cos I heard the church bell ring. He come up to me outside the church where I sits on the bench, and arst if I wanted to make a few bob…I mean, a couple of quid.'

'And what did he ask you to do?'

Griggs sniffed. 'Just told me to take a package from the doorstep of that there cottage, when I heard the church clock strike twelve, and come back and leave it under the hedge outside the church within the hour. He said if nothing was there or anyone in the cottage spoke to me, I was to clear off sharpish.'

'I see. Is there anything else you can remember about this gentleman?'

'I ain't in no trouble, am I vicar?'

'Not if you keep this conversation to yourself.'

'Righto then. Well, let me see. He sounded foreign, like. I used to be in the merchant navy and he spoke like one of them Ruskies, or Poles or such like. Never could stand those blighters, nor them strong spirits what they drank. Me having took the Pledge, that is.'

'Thank you Mr Griggs,' said Shaw, hastily mounting his bicycle. 'Please deliver the package as instructed, post haste. That is all.'

Griggs stared open mouthed as Shaw turned his bicycle in the lane.

'Here, vicar, is that it? I gets a fiver just for telling you that?'

Shaw nodded and mounted his bicycle. 'You have been most helpful Mr Griggs. Most helpful!'

Griggs continued to stare, with a puzzled expression on his face, as Shaw turned and cycled away rapidly up the lane to Elsie's cottage.

*

After he had warned Elsie to stay inside with the doors locked, Shaw scribbled a note and sealed it in an envelope addressed to Superintendent Gregory, urging Elsie to give it to him once he had arrived, assuming of course that he would. Shaw would not be drawn by Elsie's questioning on where he was going, but he noticed that she was looking out at him as he cycled up the lane towards The Larches.

Shaw rang the electric bell at the entrance, but nobody emerged from the house; after a few moments he opened the heavy wrought iron gates and cycled up the snow-covered gravel path to the main door.

After leaning his bicycle against the porch, he rang again, this time pulling the old-fashioned bell pull, and he heard the sound of the bell somewhere deep within the house. Again, nobody came. He took a deep breath and decided he had no choice but to go in. He tried the door handle, and to his surprise, it was unlocked. He stepped into the gloomy, wood-panelled hallway.

'Mrs Burward?' he called out. No answer came.

'Mr Zorard? Is anybody at home?'

Again, he heard no sound. He walked rapidly along the corridor, past the drawing room and the billiard room, and let himself in to the unlocked gun room. He walked over to the heap of blankets in the corner and looked under them. What he saw confirmed his suspicions. He made his way back along the corridor, and on the way out of the house, he tried the telephone, but it was still not working; presumably the line had not yet been mended. It would be better, he decided, to return to Elsie's cottage and telephone from there.

As he left the house he heard a scraping sound, and looked to his left to see the large, dark green painted doors of the mock-tudor garage being opened. He walked over briskly and came face to face with Zorard.

Chapter Twelve

Zorard appeared surprised, but quickly regained his composure.

'Mr Shaw,' he said brightly. 'You startled me. My apologies, there was nobody to receive you as I sent Mrs Burward home for the afternoon. As you can see, I am on my way out.'

Shaw glanced at the Rolls-Royce in the garage, which had a number of trunks and boxes visible on the back seat.

'Rather a lot of luggage for an afternoon out,' he said.

Zorard's face remained frozen in a polite smile. 'I have a number of errands to run. His Majesty's death has led to a great deal of work for me, which of course I am happy to undertake. If you will state your business, I will do my best to help you but I must leave soon.'

Shaw stepped in front of the garage doors. 'I am sorry to have to do this, Mr Zorard, but I cannot allow you to leave this property. The police are on their way and when I speak to them they will wish to detain you.'

'My dear Mr Shaw,' said Zorard, unctuously. 'I have no idea what you are talking about. I spoke to Superintendent Gregory recently, and he was confident that Ana Walters was to be charged with the killing of His Majesty.'

'I will be frank, Mr Zorard,' said Shaw. 'Certain pieces of evidence have come to light which I believe will be sufficient to convict you of the murder of King Basil and the theft of the Fenekslavian crown jewels.'

Zorard threw his head back and laughed. 'Ah, the English amateur detectives! How delightful. I have read of them in books, of course, but never met one. I am sorry to disappoint you, Mr Shaw. Whatever theories you have about me are wrong. Some men might take such accusations badly, but I will put them down to the effects of shock and confusion after the traumatic events which took place in this house. Now, if you will excuse me, I must leave.'

Zorard opened the door of the car. Shaw moved forwards into the garage, and stood in front of the vehicle's radiator. He knew that he must not let the man get away before the police arrived, but how could he stop him? He realised it was time to lay his cards on the table.

'Before you leave,' said Shaw, 'would you not like to know the whereabouts of the missing ring?'

The remark hit home. The smile disappeared from Zorard's face. 'What do you mean?' he asked.

'The ring which forms part of the crown jewels of Fenekslavia.'

'I do not know what you are talking about. The crown jewels of Fenekslavia are held in a safety deposit box in London.'

'No, Mr Zorard,' said Shaw, shaking his head. 'I have reason to believe the crown jewels are in this very motor car.'

Shaw pointed to a canvas bag on top of a suitcase on the back seat.

'I do not have any time for this nonsense,' snapped Zorard. 'Kindly step out of the way, I am leaving now.'

Shaw stood still. He realised he had to play for time. 'If you leave now you will never find the ring. Certainly it will not be left for you under the church hedge.'

An expression of shock passed momentarily over Zorard's face, but then his expression became impassive. I have him, thought Shaw.

'I have no idea what you are babbling about,' sighed Zorard. 'Get out of my way immediately.'

'No,' said Shaw, bluntly. 'I imagine your masters in Moscow will be very unhappy if you do not have the full set of jewels. The loss of an item worth fifty thousand guineas will not be taken lightly.'

The remark hit home as Shaw hoped it would.

'Moscow?' spat Zorard. 'You think I am some filthy communist?'

'I am not sure what your reasons are, but I am reasonably certain that you did kill the king.'

'How can you possibly prove this?'

Shaw sensed that the man's vanity was causing him to be curious, and he seized on the opportunity to keep him talking until help arrived. If, indeed, it was going to arrive at all.

'I think, Mr Zorard, that you did not bargain on there being snow on the ground when you carried out your plan. This made it very easy to see the evidence of certain activities around the house.'

'Go on.'

'I first became suspicious when you alleged that shots had been fired at you on the front and back steps of the house. When I went out later, I found an empty cartridge case in the snow. You claimed that you saw nobody, but the cartridge case must have been ejected from a pistol fired close by the door. It was clear from patterns in the snow that someone had been searching for it.'

'I do not see what this proves.'

'Very little in itself. But Superintendent Gregory told me that his technicians have proven that the cartridge case came from the same pistol that was used to kill King Basil.'

Zorard raised his eyebrows in surprise. 'That still is meaningless.'

'Allow me to continue,' said Shaw. 'At first I thought that whoever shot the king must have done so using the rifle which was found in the gun room. But, again thanks to the Superintendent, I learned that the king was shot with a pistol at close range.'

'Hurry up, please, Mr Shaw,' said Zorard. 'I will indulge you a little longer out of curiosity, but please do not take too long.'

'It was then my theory that somebody shot the king through the drawing room window,' said Shaw. 'But it was only later, after wracking my memory, that I realised I had not seen any footprints in the snow outside the window. It was not possible for someone to have fired from the courtyard. To have fired from anywhere else would have been, according to the Superintendent's reports, too far away. Which left only one possibility. That the king was shot from inside the room.'

'And you think that it was me who did so?' sneered Zorard.

'I know that I did not do it, it and it is highly unlikely that Mrs Burward did it.'

'Then who threw the stone through the window?'

'That was, I think, your attempt at a master stroke,' said Shaw. 'You wanted to make it look as if an assassin was outside the house and you devised an ingenious way to do this. You set up the electric-powered clay pigeon trap in such a way that it hurled a rock with a message tied to it through the gun room window, which then passed through the drawing room window, giving the impression that desperate assassins were waiting outside the house.'

'Bravo, Mr Shaw,' said Zorard sarcastically. 'And how did you deduce such a thing?'

'I believe that at some point, probably while you were supposedly putting the guns and traps away while we had gone in for tea, that you set up the trap in the gun room and laid its cable across the courtyard. Your footprints and the cable were, fortunately for you at that time, concealed by the fresh snowfall which followed. That is why you appeared to reach out of the window slightly when you said you heard somebody outside – you did not go to the window because you heard intruders – you did it to operate the mechanism of the trap.

'Concealed by the darkness of the room, you then shot the king at point blank range from within the room, standing by the window, and because it was dark, myself and Mrs Burward assumed the shot came from outside.

'You later entered the gun room, telling the rest of us to wait outside for our own protection, but really because you wanted privacy. You hid the trap under some blankets and hurriedly pulled in the cable – but by this time snow had covered it and thus it left a visible mark in the snow when pulled up. I saw the line when we caught Soames – or rather, Carter – climbing through the window, but had no understanding of what it signified until later.'

'This proves nothing,' scoffed Zorard. 'It is your word against mine. You or the Burward woman could just as easily have shot the king from within the room.'

'No, Mr Zorard,' said Shaw. 'We could not have. Remember, the same pistol was used by whoever fired at you at the front and back doors, and it could not have been used by myself or Mrs Burward because we were both in the hall when that happened.

'I believe it was you who fired the shots, to make it appear as if assassins were outside, so that nobody would leave. You left the incriminating evidence of a spent cartridge case by the back door, and another one in the living room when you shot the king. Miss Garnham was clever enough to spot that one and fortunately, she told me about it. You should have used a revolver, so that the spent cartridges remained in the chamber. I presume you did not have access to one, or you would have done so.'

'Rubbish, this is nonsense,' said Zorard, although Shaw noticed a hint of desperation in the man's voice.

'It was also foolish of you,' continued Shaw, 'to plant the pistol in Mrs Walters' handbag. It was far too obvious an attempt to incriminate her. Just as you made a similar attempt to incriminate Miss Garnham by making it appear the hunting rifle had been fired from the gun room. That was particularly pointless as you must have known that the police would check what type of gun was used to kill the king.'

Shaw saw that Zorard was at the end of his patience. He was beginning to think now that Gregory was not going to arrive. He wondered if the detective at Ipswich police station had even bothered to write down the message.

'There is just one more thing I want to know,' said Zorard.

Shaw felt a tiny vestige of hope as he realised Zorard still had a little curiosity left.

'If,' said Zorard, 'what you say is true, then why would I go to this trouble to steal jewels which are imitations? I told you before, the crown jewels are in a vault in London.'

'That was another piece of subterfuge,' said Shaw. 'You needed an excuse as to why you were so willing to give up the priceless crown jewels of your country without a fight. You also knew that when the police eventually arrived, they would be less likely to take interest in the loss of some worthless fakes. So you invented the story about the real jewels being left in a safety deposit box in London when you arrived in this country.'

'You fool,' said Zorard, shaking his head. 'The police are meeting me in London tomorrow morning to transfer the crown jewels from the safety deposit box to the Tower of London where they will be kept until the next coronation.'

'I very much doubt it,' said Shaw. 'You see, I do not think there is a fake set of jewels. Why on earth would you bother to take such a thing when fleeing for your lives from Fenekslavia with only the luggage you could carry?

'I believe you may indeed have a safety deposit box in London, but that there are no crown jewels within it. You know that this subterfuge will be revealed when the police ask the staff at the Ritz for evidence that the deposit was made. It was the real jewels that you placed on the front step and you managed to convince the police that Ana Walters had taken them, when in fact you had concealed them in the house in the few moments before Sergeant Carter revealed his true identity. This is your first chance to flee the country before the deception is revealed.'

For the first time, Shaw noticed that Zorard looked genuinely worried.

'These are interesting theories,' said Zorard. 'But you cannot know that the jewels are not fake.'

'I can and I do, Mr Zorard,' insisted Shaw. 'You see, that was another mistake that you made – breaking into Miss Garnham's cottage and leaving a note demanding the restoration of the ring. I assume at some point you realised the ring was missing and guessed, correctly, that Miss

Garnham had it. I noticed the handwriting was similar to that on the note that was thrown with the rock through the drawing room window, by the way. I knew that meant the jewels must be genuine, as why would anyone go to the trouble of stealing them and making threats to kill for imitations? If anybody else – Bolshevik agents, for example – had stolen the jewels, they would surely have noticed the subterfuge by now. My suspicions were confirmed when I had the ring examined by a jeweller in Great Netley.'

'This ring…' said Zorard, in a tone of forced nonchalance, 'does Miss Garnham have it about her person?'

'No, Mr Zorard, she did, but she does not now. She complied with your instructions to leave a package on the front step of her cottage.'

Zorard now appeared confused. Beads of sweat appeared on his forehead, which he hastily wiped away with the back of his hand.

'Do not worry, Mr Zorard,' said Shaw. 'Mr Griggs – the gentleman you recently commissioned for your errand – carried out your requests to the letter. But the package he will be leaving under the church hedge will not contain the ring, only a piece of make-weight junk which I substituted for the genuine article.

'Although you had your face covered when you spoke to him, your clothes and accent will probably be sufficient to satisfy the police that it was you with whom he spoke. By the way, I believe you owe him a pound for his trouble – if you give it to me I shall be happy to pass it on.'

'Enough!' snapped Zorard. Shaw's eyebrows lifted in surprise as he saw that the man had grabbed a shotgun from the back seat of the Rolls-Royce. Shaw raised his hands and stepped back as Zorard nudged the weapon into his midriff.

'Enough of this blabbering,' he snarled. 'You are very clever. Everything you say is true, about what I did. But it does not matter because I will soon be away from this godforsaken place before anyone has a chance to stop me. Tell me where the ring is now, or I shoot you dead.'

'If you shoot me,' said Shaw, struggling to remain calm, 'you will never find the ring.'

'Very well then, you will die,' said Zorard, moving back the safety catch of the shotgun.

Shaw realised the end was near, and that, for some inexplicable reason, it had not pleased Almighty God to send anyone to his rescue. He decided to make a final attempt to delay what now seemed inevitable.

'At least tell me why,' said Shaw. 'Before you kill me. Why did you kill your own king? For money, I suppose.'

The remark stung Zorard. 'For money? Of course not. I did it to protect the crown of Fenekslavia. From that…pompous buffoon.'

'He was still your sovereign lord,' protested Shaw.

'He forfeited that sacred duty!' exclaimed Zorard. 'Leaving his people in their hour of need, tricking me into helping him escape to England by saying that he would return to Fenekslavia, and then changing his mind. It was all so he could live here in this, this, indolent country, with that strumpet, that ridiculous *kurvecka* from the music halls.'

Zorard paused, and Shaw wondered briefly what a *kurvecka* was, although he had a good idea what it might mean. Then Zorard continued with his diatribe.

'I was even willing to accept his decision to stay here, thinking that one day he might be persuaded to return to his homeland. But when he decided he would marry this…Elsie…it was too much. I could not risk that they might have children.'

'Why does it matter if he had further issue?' asked Shaw in confusion.

'Surely you know enough history,' replied Zorard, 'even of your own country, to know what happens if there are two rival claimants to a kingdom. I could not risk it. The king's son, Prince Stefan, is and must remain the only rightful heir.'

'I see,' said Shaw. 'I see it all now. I was foolish enough to believe that the motivation was money. But it was power. How old is Prince Stefan?'

'Nineteen,' said Zorard, proudly. 'I have always been interested in the boy, knowing that his father was not up to the task of kingship. He reminds me much of his grandfather, the late King Miroslav the Third, of blessed memory. He was a true Fenek king and one I was proud to serve as a young officer. But his son…a vain poppinjay, a puppet of the Austro-Hungarians. He is better off dead.'

Shaw saw a gleam of mania in Zorard's eyes as the man looked into the middle distance towards some imagined future. The shotgun, however, was still held uncomfortably close to his midriff.

'Once we have assembled our allies,' continued Zorard, 'we will return in glory to drive the communists from our land. The prince will reach his majority in a couple of years, and will be crowned king, with the ancient crown jewels as it has always been.'

'And you, I take it, will assume the title of some sort of Regent in the meantime?' asked Shaw.

'Of course. I will guide and nurture the boy. That is why I had to got to such lengths to make sure the blame for the king's death was put on others. Prince Stefan would never trust me if he knew the truth.'

'And you will take power purely as a temporary measure before he comes of age?' asked Shaw.

A red flush of anger crossed Zorard's face. 'You imply I wish the crown for myself. Preposterous! All over Europe, men like me are coming to the fore. Strong men, who will drive away both the filth of communism and the weakness of sentimental liberals like you Englishmen. We will respect the office of our traditional leaders, but if they fail us, like King Basil, they will be swept away. You have tried my patience long enough, priest. Your time is up. Prepare yourself.'

Shaw dropped to his knees and clasped his hands in prayer in front of him. He fixed Zorard's eyes in a steely gaze, and then spoke clearly and firmly.

'May God forgive you. May He forgive us both.'

Zorard aimed the shotgun at Shaw's head. There was a loud bang and a blast of displaced air, then Shaw fell backwards onto the snow-covered drive, which was spattered with droplets of blood.

Zorard screamed in pain and dropped the shotgun on the ground, clutching at his right hand, which was pouring blood onto his white shirt-cuff.

It took Shaw a moment to realise that he was still alive. He groped his way back onto his knees and turned to see a woman standing a few feet away. It was Elsie Garnham. With a steady hand, she was pointing a small pistol at Zorard.

Zorard laughed and then winced in pain. 'You…you expect to stop me with that thing? A child's toy, for the theatre.'

'It's a point two-two saloon pistol, Zorard,' said Elsie. 'Not good for much more than shooting tin cans on stage, I'll admit, but if you make another move I'll get you between the eyes with it.'

Zorard spoke with a hollow, rasping sound. 'If you could kill me you would have done so already.'

Shaw heard the plop, plop of large drops of blood as they dripped from the man's hand onto the compacted snow.

No,' said Elsie. 'I could have killed you at any time in the last few minutes from where I was hiding. I followed Mr Shaw here because I had my suspicions about you and I was right. I wanted to hear you admit what you'd done, and you did. Now put your hands up and move away from that shotgun.'

'Stop right there!', a man bellowed from a few feet away behind Shaw. He turned to see that it was Superintendent Gregory, who had grabbed Elsie and was attempting to seize her pistol. Realising his opportunity, Zorard grabbed the shotgun and held it unsteadily in front of him. Shaw realised that at this range, he could kill or at least maim all three of them.

Without thinking, he grabbed the barrel of the shotgun and jerked it upwards; Zorard's grip was weakened by the injury to his hand. The gun went off with a deafening explosion and Shaw felt a hot blast of air singe his eyebrows, but the shot went harmlessly into the air.

Zorard released his grip on the weapon and slumped backwards onto the snow. Shaw stood up and saw a neat bullet hole perfectly placed between the man's now lifeless eyes. He turned to see that Sergeant Carter and Superintendent Gregory had finally managed to remove the pistol from Elsie's hands, but it was too late – the Annie Oakley of England had, as she had promised, found her mark.

'I've spoken to a solicitor,' said Keir, drawing heavily on a Woodbine and pushing back his hair out of his eyes. He stood in the doorway of the little bedroom in the flat above the café. Ana tucked in Sofia's blankets to the sides of the cot and looked up at her husband as he spoke.

'He thinks we've got a good case for wrongful arrest, for both of us. It'll cost us a fortune but we can't let the police get away with this sort of thing. Father's writing to the Howard League for Penal Reform as well.'

'No,' said Ana, simply.

'What do you mean, "no"?' asked Keir. 'They would have had you hanged for murder if that vicar hadn't worked out what really happened.'

'I do not believe so,' said Ana. 'The truth would have come out. There was not enough evidence against me. And besides, they were right to arrest me. I stole.'

'You stole to help feed the hungry. That's different.'

'It is still wrong. I realise that now.'

'A few knives and forks,' said Keir, slightly exasperated. 'They kept you in that cell for two days!'

'Do you have any idea,' said Ana, 'what the police in Fenekslavia would have done to me had I been arrested there?'

Keir for once was silent. Ana stood up and put her arms around her husband's waist.

'Yes they kept me in a cell. But they did not beat me. And they let me go even though they could have sent me to prison. This is something that could never happen in my country. I do not wish you to complain about it.'

'But…they have no right…' protested Keir, weakly. Once more, he glimpsed in his wife's eyes the steely resolve bred of generations of hardship and oppression.

'Let us just live our life and appreciate what we have,' said Ana, looking down at Sofia. 'There are many Zorards in the world, more and more each day. One day, I think, even the quiet people of England may have to go to war against them. Let us enjoy the peace for now.'

*

'Your Royal Highness,' said Mrs Shaw, curtseying deeply to the handsome young man in military uniform in front of her. The fresh duelling scar on his angular cheek seemed only to enhance his good looks rather than detract from them. Shaw bowed from the neck and then shook the offered hand of Prince Stefan, or to give him his full title, His Royal Highness the Prince Stefan of Fenekslavia in Exile.

'Thank you so much for coming Mr Shaw,' said the prince. 'I trust the service was not too unfamiliar for you?'

'No sir,' replied Shaw. 'I have a passing knowledge of the Orthodox funerary rites, after having done some research on their history while at Cambridge.'

'And you, Mrs Shaw,' said the prince, 'there were not too many bowings and crossings for you, I hope?'

Mrs Shaw appeared tongue-tied, and blushed like a nervous schoolgirl.

One of the two official-looking men – Special Branch bodyguards, Shaw assumed – whispered something into the prince's ear.

'I am sorry, Mr and Mrs Shaw. You must excuse me. I am told the cortege is now to depart for the Necropolis station, and then to Brookwood cemetery.'

'Brookwood?' asked Shaw. 'I assumed His Majesty's remains would be buried in Fenekslavia.'

'They will be, God willing,' said the prince. 'One day

he will be reburied in his homeland, but for now, we must wait – and fight – for that time to come. But thank you, once again, for your brave actions in this most regrettable affair. Had you not intervened, it is possible that Zorard would have seized the throne of Fenekslavia.'

'Your Royal Highness,' murmured Shaw and bowed again as the prince walked away, with a jingle of spurs and a rattle from the highly polished sabre strapped to his uniform.

Shaw and his wife followed, and stepped out of the dark little Orthodox church, tucked away in a residential corner of London's West Kensington district, the haunt of White Russian émigrés and others forced to flee to England as Bolshevism continued its slow encroachment across Europe. There being no Fenekslavian church in England in which to conduct a royal funeral, this was considered the next best thing by the small band of Fenekslavian exiles who were now guiding the prince.

Curious locals and press-men were held back on the pavements by police constables; there was a moment of silence and then some shouted orders in Fenekslavian, salutes were exchanged, boots crunched on gravel, and the bearded priest waved a censer in front of the hearse. Incense blended with the breath of the horses, stamping in the chilly air, and rose up to disappear over the soot-stained terraced houses. Then the cortege moved slowly away towards Waterloo station, for the final journey to Brookwood.

'He's awfully good looking, isn't he?' said Mrs Shaw, as she watched the small procession depart. 'The prince I mean.'

'I suppose so,' said Shaw. 'I fear, however, that his youthful enthusiasm to regain the throne may be misplaced.'

'Oh don't be so gloomy, Lucian dear,' said Mrs Shaw. 'Why on earth would the Fenekslavians want some dreary communists in charge, when they could have someone as dashing as Prince Stefan? They'll soon come to their senses.'

'Perhaps,' said Shaw. Inwardly, however, he saw only the slow *exeunt* of kings and priests from the stage of Europe, purged by the seemingly remorseless rise of secular demagogues cast in the mould of Zorard.

A woman with a black veil over her face approached them, accompanied by a small, dapper looking man of Levantine appearance. The woman pulled back the veil and Shaw saw that it was Elsie Garnham.

'Miss Garnham,' said Shaw, accepting the woman's black-gloved hand.

'How do you do, vicar, and Mrs Shaw,' said Elsie. 'This my agent, Mr Samuels,' she said, indicating the man next to her. 'He came along to give moral support.'

The diminutive man removed his hat and unctuously shook Shaw's hands with both of his own. 'Good to know you, Reverend, and Mrs…Reverend. Monty Samuels, agent to the stars. My card.' He thrust a small business card into Shaw's top coat pocket and patted it.

'I thought you would be travelling with the cortege,' said Shaw, stepping back slightly from the rather too close and perfumed figure of Mr Samuels.

'Not likely, vicar,' said Elsie. 'That lot would rather forget I ever existed.'

'And I'm here to make sure that doesn't happen, my dear,' said Samuels. 'Tell them the good news,' he added.

'Monty's arranged a tour of America,' said Elsie, with a touch of pride. 'Seems they've already heard about the murder over there and they can't get enough of it.'

'"The sharpshooter and the charlatan – how one

woman foiled a murderer."' Samuels wrote an imaginary headline in the air with his hands as he spoke. 'That's the angle we're going for. The Yanks love that sort of thing.' He turned to Shaw. 'How about you, Reverend? I'm happy to represent you and all. I've heard you're a bit of an amateur detective, so how about this for a headline: "I am the Way, the Sleuth, and the Life."'

Samuels did not notice the look of distaste on Shaw's face, as the impresario was distracted by the gaggle of newspapermen who had realised who Elsie was. Her face, now unveiled, had been splashed across all the tabloid newspapers when the murder of King Basil had been made public a couple of days previously.

Samuels put a protective arm around Elsie and ushered her away to a waiting motor car as he called out to the pressmen. 'Interviews at the Bayswater Hotel in ten minutes,' he said. 'Miss Garnham is sailing for New York this evening so don't hang about.'

A man in a raincoat pushed forward to Shaw and his wife and raised a camera; they were momentarily dazzled by the light of a flashbulb. 'Care to make a statement, vicar?' wheedled the man, in a strong cockney accent.

A policeman stepped in front of the reporter and Shaw realised it was time to go; the crowd had spotted him and he had no desire to recount his experiences to the gutter press.

'What extraordinary people,' said Mrs Shaw. 'Do let's go, Lucian. Our train's at three and I've had rather enough of strange men pushing and shoving us about.'

Shaw looked in vain for a taxi but just then, a large saloon car pulled up beside them on the pavement. The rear door opened. 'May I offer you a lift, Mr and Mrs Shaw?' said a voice from within.

Shaw looked into the car and saw Superintendent

Gregory. 'We'll be passing Liverpool Street station,' said the policeman. 'I assume that's where you're going?'

With relief, Shaw and his wife sat down in the car and soon they were being driven swiftly through the London streets, past pavements thronged with Christmas shoppers.

'I've been put in charge of royal protection duties for Prince Stefan while he's in England,' said Gregory, 'and this time there won't be any mistakes. I've got my best men on this and he'll be looked after properly until he goes back to his college in Germany.'

'You did a good job, Mr Shaw,' he continued, 'if you don't mind my saying so. 'You kept Zorard talking until we had time to get there. If you hadn't done that he would have been on the continent by now and out of our reach. I'm only sorry we didn't get there sooner.'

'I fear that Mr Zorard would have eventually met the same fate, even if it was at the hands of the hangman rather than Miss Garnham,' said Shaw.

'Oh I'm sure of that,' said Gregory. 'What I'm sorry about is what you had to go through, not him.'

'It is the others I am concerned for,' said Shaw.

'Others?' asked Gregory. 'You mean Elsie Garnham and Ana Walters, I take it?'

Shaw nodded.

'Elsie won't face any charges, she had no choice but to shoot Zorard, we all saw that. I've told her she might have to cut her American tour short though, as there will have to be an enquiry.'

'And Mrs Walters?'

'We let her go with a caution. Pinching knives and forks is still a crime, but in the grand scheme of things we've got more important matters to worry about.

'I'll say goodbye then, Mr Shaw, Mrs Shaw,' said

Gregory, as the car pulled up outside Liverpool Street station. Before they got out Gregory placed his hand on Shaw's arm. 'Oh, and remember, both of you,' he said in a low voice, 'that although the murder's been made public, the business with the foreign agents is being kept out of this.

'We've also heard rumours over the air that the Fenekslavian intelligence officer who planned the assassination has been shot. Seems the Reds weren't happy that Zorard killed the king before they did. Anyway, the Home Office does not want word getting around that agents of a foreign power were able to even attempt an assassination on British soil. And nor do I, for that matter.'

'I quite understand, Superintendent,' said Shaw. 'Thank you for the lift, and goodbye.'

'Goodbye, Mr and Mrs Shaw, and a Merry Christmas to you.'

The driver slammed the door and within seconds the car had pulled out into the heavy traffic on Bishopsgate. As they walked over to the station, Mrs Shaw looked down in distaste at the grey slush beneath her feet.

'Snow never looks clean in London, does it?' she said. 'I can't wait to get back to Suffolk, where it stays pure and white for ages.'

'Perhaps,' said Shaw. For a moment he recalled the red-spattered snow when Zorard had been shot, which for an instant he had thought was the last thing he would see on earth.

Somewhere on the concourse a brass band was playing, probably the Salvation Army, thought Shaw. After a moment, he recognised the tune: *Tempus Adest Floridum*, or as it was better known, *Good King Wenceslas.* He smiled and took his wife's arm as they walked across the concourse to the train that would take them home.

Other Reverend Shaw books by Hugh Morrison

A Third Class Murder

An antiques dealer is found robbed and murdered in a third class train compartment on a remote Suffolk branch line. Reverend Shaw, is concerned that the police have arrested the wrong man, and begins his own investigation.

The Wooden Witness

After finding the battered corpse of a spiritualist medium at an archaeological site on the Suffolk coast, the Reverend Lucian Shaw is thrust into a dark and deadly mystery involving ancient texts and modern technology.

Death on the Night Train

When the Reverend Lucian Shaw is summoned to Scotland by a mysterious telegram, he gets caught up in a deadly conspiracy reaching to the highest levels of government.

Murder in Act Three

When village gossip Joan Hexham is killed during an amateur dramatics performance, everyone assumes it is an unfortunate accident – except Reverend Lucian Shaw. But can he prove it was murder, before the killer strikes again?

Murder at Evensong

A famous left-wing cleric – 'the most hated parson in England' as the newspapers call him – falls to his death during Evensong at Midchester Cathedral. Reverend Shaw is determined to find his assailant – but at what cost to himself?